"It's Funny, Really," Johanna Said, Forcing A Nervous Laugh.

"Acting so childish over a little kiss. For heaven's sake, I was married for ten years. We've known each other most of our lives. Tell me I'm being silly. Tell me it was just a kiss, Michael."

"If that's what you want to hear," he said.

She looked into his eyes. They were asking a question she wasn't quite prepared to answer. Not yet. "Yes," she said. "It is."

"Then, you're being silly, Johanna. It was just a kiss."

Dear Reader,

There's so much in store for you this month from Silhouette Desire! First, don't miss *Cowboys Don't Cry* by Anne McAllister. Not only is this a *Man of the Month*— it's also the first book in her CODE OF THE WEST series. Look for the next two books in this series later in the year.

Another terrific miniseries, FROM HERE TO MATERNITY by Elizabeth Bevarly, also begins, with *A Dad Like Daniel*. These delightful stories about the joys of unexpected parenthood continue in April and June!

For those of you who like a touch of the otherworldly, take a look at Judith McWilliams's *Anything's Possible!* And the month is completed by Carol Devine's *A Man of the Land,* Audra Adams's *His Brother's Wife,* and *Truth or Dare* by Caroline Cross.

Next month, we celebrate the 75th *Man of the Month* with a very special Desire title, **That Burke Man** by **Diana Palmer**. It's part of her LONG, TALL TEXANS series, and I know you won't want to miss it!

Happy reading!

Lucia Macro
Senior Editor

Please address questions and book requests to:
Silhouette Reader Service
U.S.: 3010 Walden Ave., P.O. Box 1325, Buffalo, NY 14269
Canadian: P.O. Box 609, Fort Erie, Ont. L2A 5X3

AUDRA
ADAMS
HIS BROTHER'S WIFE

SILHOUETTE *Desire*®
Published by Silhouette Books
America's Publisher of Contemporary Romance

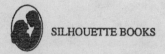

SILHOUETTE BOOKS

ISBN 0-373-05912-4

HIS BROTHER'S WIFE

Printed in U.S.A.

Books by Audra Adams

Silhouette Desire

Blue Chip Bride #532
People Will Talk #592
Home Sweet Home #695
Devil or Angel #738
Rich Girl, Bad Boy #839
His Brother's Wife #912

AUDRA ADAMS

loves to dream up her characters' stories while lying on the beach on hot summer days. Luckily, her Jersey-shore home offers her the opportunity to indulge in her fantasies.

She believes that falling in love is one of the most memorable experiences in a person's life. Young or old, male or female, we can all relate to those exquisitely warm feelings. She knows that stories of romance enable us to tap into that hidden pleasure and relive it through characters.

An incurable romantic, Audra is in love with love, and hopes to share that optimism with each and every one of her readers.

To the women in my life—
my mother, Josephine Bluni,
my aunt, Anne Palmieri,
my sisters, Grace Scheno and Barbara Parisi—
and this mystery called family

One

"Here we are, lady."

Johanna Ross stared at the house in disbelief. This couldn't be the place! She glanced down at the address on the scrap of paper held tightly in her fist, then back again to the shiny brass numbers blazoned on the second of four columns of the majestic gray Southern colonial.

They were the same.

The taxi driver exited the car and popped the trunk before opening the back passenger door for her.

"I can't believe it," she said, more to herself than to him.

"Pretty nice place," he said with a nod toward the house.

"Yes." She dug into her jeans pocket for her money. "Too nice."

Johanna handed the driver the money, and he handed her the duffel bag. She felt her face turn red as he counted out the rumpled bills. There wasn't much of a tip. "Sorry," she said.

The cab driver shrugged good-naturedly and motioned toward the house, which to Johanna's eyes looked more like a mansion. "Maybe your luck'll change," he said with a grin.

"Maybe."

She lifted the duffel bag over her shoulder and waved a halfhearted goodbye to the driver as she made her way up the concrete walkway to the main entrance.

Johanna took a deep breath as she glanced up at the sky. It was a perfect September day.

New beginnings.

If she'd been told a year ago that she would be living in the same house with Michael Ross, she'd have been struck dumb.

She wondered, not for the first time, what Jeff would have thought of all of this. He'd approve, she decided, and make some offhand comment about the fact that Michael could afford it. Although outwardly contemptuous of his brother's success, her husband harbored a deep and abiding pride and respect for Michael's accomplishments and would never fail to defend—or even brag about—Michael to other people. But never to Michael.

Having been an only child of older parents, Johanna never really understood the rivalry between the two, but theirs had been the quintessential sibling love-hate relationship...and for more than ten years she had been caught right smack in the middle of it.

The brothers had kept in touch, of course. Those short, overly friendly, obligatory family phone calls on birthdays and holidays. How long had it been since she'd seen Michael? Aside from the funeral, which remained a blur to this day, Joanna recalled the last time they'd all been together had been Christmas Day five years ago. They'd flown in from California for the holiday to visit her in-laws, Arlene and Steve Ross.

It had been uncomfortable for her that year. Her parents had passed away not too long before, and while everyone was very sensitive to her, being back in the old neighborhood and seeing new people living in her old house next door had been very painful. Yet Jeff had wanted to come home, and as usual, she had acquiesced.

Michael had come alone. Didn't stay long either, as she recalled. Her stomach had been in knots the whole time. She'd avoided him as best she could, avoided those blue eyes of his that saw too much. But Johanna remembered how he'd looked. Tall, dark, impeccably dressed in his white oxford shirt and navy Brooks Brothers suit. Stark contrast to Jeff's tattered jeans and studded leather vest.

But then, that had always been the case between the two. The competition was clear and sometimes painful to watch. Whatever Michael pursued, Jeff chased after the opposite—with a vengeance.

Johanna unknowingly shook her head. She'd gone deaf listening to Jeff complain about how Michael was conservative to a fault, while *he* was the talented one, wild, impulsive, always ready to act on a dare....

And wasn't that exactly why she'd run off and married him?

No, that wasn't why, she'd told herself but not him. Never him. Until that night. Johanna shivered from a cold within. She shook it off. She was bone-tired of ruminating about the whys or wherefores of the last ten years of her life.

That was the reason she was here—to put the past behind her.

She thought about ringing the doorbell, then changed her mind. She wasn't quite ready to face Michael. Dropping the duffel bag between her feet, Johanna jammed her right hand into her jeans pocket in search of her cigarettes. She checked the pack. Only two left. Just as well. Unlike Jeff, Michael was a nonsmoker, and she was certain that he would disapprove of her bad habit—one she had successfully quit until Jeff's leftover bills had begun pouring in one after another in a deluge of debt she wasn't sure she'd ever outswim.

She lit the cigarette and inhaled deeply, putting out the match with a shake of her wrist. She was just about to drop it on the ground when she stopped short. Mustn't dirty Michael's porch, she admonished herself, slipping the dead match into her pocket for disposal later.

It wasn't supposed to relax her, she knew, but the first drag always did wonders for her nerves. And she *was* nervous, more than she could ever remember being.

Which was absurd, of course. Johanna had known Michael most of her life. Since she was twelve, to be exact, and she and her parents had made what she'd hoped was their last move next door to the Rosses. Within a year, she'd developed a friendship with Jeff and a *major* adolescent crush on Michael.

More than a crush. By senior year in high school it had developed into full-blown love. At least, she was as in love as a seventeen-year-old could be on a hot summer night ...

But then, that was *old* news. Why, the thought of that night hardly made her wince with shame anymore, as it had for too many years. She'd outgrown her adolescent overreaction during her marriage to Jeff. And even though she and Michael kept each other at arm's length, they had certainly gotten along well enough as in-laws.

Michael Ross, brother-in-law. She grinned and shook her head. It was still next to impossible to think of him that way.

Even now. Especially now.

Yet, there was really no reason for her to be this uptight. He'd always been someone she trusted, and nothing had happened to change that. Besides, this was a mutually beneficial arrangement. She was doing him a favor by accepting his position as housekeeper, and Lord knew that he was doing one for her in return.

No, don't think about that. Thinking about being broke and homeless made her depressed.

She took a last drag and looked around for a place to put out the cigarette. A stone bed was off to the left, fitting in the picture-perfect landscaping as though an artist had blended it for color, shape and style into the wooded setting. Rubbing the cigarette against the back of the stone, she shredded it and buried the remains under some wood chips. Feeling like a thief in the night, she stood upright and edged her way to the front door.

It was time to bite the bullet. She pressed the bell and waited, quietly listening to the chimes within. When no one answered, she tried again. And again. It was obvious he wasn't home. Where was he? She distinctly remembered leaving a message on his machine with the exact time she would be arriving. She checked her watch. Three o'clock. Right on time.

Pressing the doorbell once again to no avail, Johanna tapped her foot. She had a good mind to leave, but as she caught sight of the duffel bag, she knew there was nowhere else for her to go. She'd played out all her options, meager as they were.

No, this was it. All her earthly goods were sitting at her feet, and that was the cold, hard truth of the matter. Some clothes, a few books, her tapes. The money she had frugally squirreled away over the years was gone. Jeff had spent it—on what, she still didn't have a clue. But she could have fixed that, just as she'd always fixed everything.

If only it hadn't rained that night.

If only they hadn't argued.

If only she had taken the keys away from him....

If only.

A light breeze caught her, cooling the sheen of perspiration around her hairline, jolting her back to the present, away from the the horrible memories of that night...the police...the wrecked car...the secret she'd kept from his family...

Enough! she screamed silently. She had put this all behind her, hadn't she? It was time to go forward, to move, to change, to make a new life for herself. Back here. Back home in New Jersey. At Michael's.

That is, if she could ever get inside.

Checking her watch again, Johanna tried to put a lid on the steam building inside her. What did Michael expect her to do? Stand here all day waiting for him? She grabbed the knob to rattle it in frustration, and to her surprise, the door opened.

"How do you like that?" she asked herself, then lifted her duffel bag and let herself in.

The foyer was cool, with only a shadow of afternoon light filtering down from the cathedral ceiling skylights overhead. She glanced up at the streaks of sunlight and smiled, the first genuine smile she'd allowed herself in days.

This might not be so bad, after all, she thought, as she took three baby steps forward and spun around.

Michael's house. It was magnificent. Bigger and more expansive than anything her mother-in-law could have described. Arlene had said he had more room than he'd ever need, and she certainly hadn't exaggerated. The place was huge. The living room was to the right, the dining room to the left, both with thick, luxurious champagne carpeting. A crystal teardrop chandelier hung down from the highest point in the ceiling, casting a rainbow prism of light on the marble floor of the foyer.

It was perfect, as far as she could tell from this vantage point. There was only one tiny, little problem.

It was empty.

No furniture.

Not a stick.

Johanna wondered about that. Michael had lived here going on two years now. She remembered Jeff playfully mimicking his parents as they bragged about the place while it was being built. He obviously could afford to furnish it, yet he'd chosen not to.

Why?

She left her duffel bag in the foyer and followed the hallway into a large, airy kitchen. Windows abounded, with double French doors opening out onto a redwood deck. The work area had the usual appliances with countertops galore. A butcher-block island sat in the center of it all, accessorized with a ceiling rack of hanging copper pots and pans—all shiny, clean . . . and unused.

The kitchen blended into a den rich with chocolate carpeting. A stone fireplace graced the corner of the room, which again contained nothing, save for a stereo system on the floor in the opposite corner and a beat-up old burnt orange couch that looked like he'd bought it at a fire sale.

Johanna shook her head. How could he live like this? The house reminded her of a blank canvas just waiting for the right artist's touch. Maybe Arlene had been right. Hard as it was to believe, maybe Michael really did need help.

Light from the skylights followed her as she climbed the stairway to the second level. Four doors faced her, two to either side of the stairway. She made a choice, turned left and checked out a smaller room—empty again, save for the royal blue carpeting. At the end of this side of the hall was another door, and without hesitation, Johanna opened it.

This room was furnished. A king-size brass bed dominated the center of the room, opposite a smaller version of the fireplace in the den. There was also a dresser, an armoire, end tables, an oriental fan overhead, and light, light, light from the four skylights and French doors, filling the room with a warm glow. Clothes were strewn on the bed, and the walk-in closet door was open.

She was just about to exit when she heard a sound, and as she turned in its direction, Johanna noticed another door slightly ajar. A prickly feeling rose up her spine as she moved toward it. With one hand, she tipped the door open.

He stood at the sink, his body still glistening from the shower, a towel wrapped around his middle. Half of his face was covered with shaving cream, the other half being efficiently shaved. His hair was wet and combed back from his forehead.

Johanna watched silently as he finished shaving, feeling like an intruder, a voyeur, yet unable to move or speak.

He was, in a word, magnificent. She was, in another word, overwhelmed.

When had this happened? When had Michael become this...man? He'd always worn clothes well, but he'd been tall and more on the thin side. All that had changed. His body was well toned, muscular, his shoulders broad, his skin lightly tanned and smooth. She felt her throat go dry and swallowed audibly.

Michael's hand halted in midair. His peripheral vision caught sight of her. Turning, he stared for an inordinately long moment.

"Hello, Michael."

"Who the hell . . . ?" His steel blue eyes, always startling, grew wider with surprise. *"Johanna?"*

She knew she'd changed since they'd last seen each other, but the extent of his astonishment was daunting. Johanna felt the heat of embarrassment rise to her face. "I-I'll just wait . . . leave—"

"You look so . . . different."

"So do you."

Michael glanced down at himself, realizing for the first time how he was dressed—or undressed. He grinned, then looked back up at her. Their eyes met, and Johanna saw all the old arrogance there. She felt a tiny blip in her stomach.

"How are you?" he asked softly.

Johanna nodded imperceptibly. "Fine."

He smiled. It was a nice smile. She'd forgotten how nice.

"I just got back from a run. I wasn't expecting you until next Sunday," he said.

"No, *this* Sunday."

"Next."

"This."

"I beg to differ," he said as he wiped the remainder of the shaving cream off his face.

"You can beg all you want. But I left a message on your machine. This Sunday afternoon, three o'clock."

"I didn't get it."

"Oh. Is it a problem?" she asked.

"No. No. Of course not." Michael slipped past her, walking into the middle of the bedroom, only steps from her. "We'll make do."

"Make do?" she asked.

"Forget it. Why don't you wait for me downstairs?" he said as he disappeared into the walk-in closet and returned with a pair of slacks and a shirt draped over his arm.

"But, Michael—"

"I'm about to get dressed, Johanna. If you want to watch," he said, shrugging, "it's okay with me." He reached for the knot in the towel.

Johanna shut her gaping mouth. Patience had never been one of his virtues. Even as a young man, he'd had a special talent for putting people in their place with just a look or a gesture.

There was an air about Michael. He exuded indifference, from his one-length, too long, dark brown hair that fell across his forehead to his authoritative attitude. Yet, at the same time, his blue eyes shone with keen intelligence, as if he were observing, dissecting, evaluating all that entered his line of vision. His mind seemed to race ahead of everyone else's. By the time one subject became clear, he was on to the next.

He raised an eyebrow and wiggled the knot in the towel. "Well, Johanna? What's it going to be?"

She walked around him to the door. "I'll wait for you downstairs."

For old times' sake, Michael chuckled just loud enough for her to hear. Just to annoy her. He used to tease the hell out of her back in the old days. But then the grin faded.

Johanna.

He sat on the edge of the bed, took a deep breath and let it out slowly in an attempt to bring his pulse back to normal. Sure, she'd taken him by surprise, but there was more to it than that. The person standing in his doorway was definitely *not* the person he had expected to see, this Sunday *or* next.

Johanna hadn't been his bratty next-door neighbor for many years, he'd known that. He'd watched her grow up. He'd watched her mature. He'd even watched her marry his brother. But despite all that, Johanna still had seemed so sweet and innocent to him, a combination of bravado and

vulnerability. And that image was frozen in his mind...
exactly as she'd looked the night of the block party.

Whoa! Mikey, my boy, calm down. *That* one's older than
the dinosaurs! Keep that memory where it belongs—locked,
hidden, *safe* in your own head.

Deal with the here. Deal with the now.

But the *now* wasn't much better, he thought as he continued dressing. He hadn't been fooling. He hadn't recognized her.

Her hair was softer, longer, blondish, even stylish... and
she had put on some healthy weight. The scrawny, anorexic
waif look was gone. Yes, she had certainly changed quite a
bit in the five years since he'd last seen her.

Suddenly, Johanna was the woman he'd always imagined she'd become.

Better.

He didn't know if he was ready to deal with Johanna as a
woman. The change was too... dramatic.

Then again, he mused, *any* change at all would have been
an improvement.

He remembered that Christmas at his parents' house. It
had been a long time between visits with her and Jeff.
Though they'd kept in touch, by that time in their lives, he
and his brother had gravitated to keeping a healthy distance from each other. He knew Jeff's reasons for the es-
trangement. They had started in high school when Michael
won the scholarship and Jeff had flunked out.

But Jeff—he hoped—had no idea about Michael's reasons.

Their parents had tried to pretend they were all one happy
family, but the visits were strained, and after that particular holiday season, Michael had made it his business to be
busy whenever future invitations came.

And now Jeff was gone....

Thoughts of the accident still plagued him, as if he should have been there, as if he could have prevented it in some way. Which was foolish, of course. He lived three thousand miles away and had a distinctly different life-style. Yet the guilt survived all his rationalizations. It was a natural growth, he supposed, from the guilt he felt about Johanna and the life she'd led with Jeff. All the feelings were jumbled, mixed up and so long in the making that even he couldn't sort them out. He only knew that in some very basic ways, he was responsible.

Well, he hadn't had the means or ability to do anything about what happened then, but he sure as hell did now. Michael wanted to right so many wrongs—for Johanna, for his brother, for himself.

And now was his chance.

He found her in the kitchen, leaning against the counter, munching on a piece of cheese.

"I hope you don't mind," she said. "I'm starving."

"Help yourself," he replied. "Though I'm afraid there's not much to eat around here."

"There's not much of anything around here," she said with a grin.

Michael reached into the refrigerator and took out a can of soda. "I was hoping you'd take charge of that." He popped the can and motioned to the den.

"Sure, I'd love to help, but why haven't you furnished the place?"

"No time."

"You could have hired an interior decorator."

"I tried that. It didn't work." His blue eyes turned opaque, and he focused his attention on the can of soda. "Want some?"

"Yes, please," she said. "I've a feeling there's more to that story. What happened, Michael?" When he didn't answer, she leaned forward. "Come on, Michael. Tell."

He poured half the can of soda into a tumbler and handed it to her. "Let's just say she was more interested in moving herself in than any new furniture."

"Did you date her?" Now, why in the world did she ask that?

"Yes."

"What was her name?"

"It doesn't matter."

"Did you go out with her for a long time?" *Johanna, stop it!*

"No."

"Major problems?" Johanna felt her face flame with embarrassment at her persistence.

"You could say that."

"Such as..."

"Such as nothing important. It's over."

Johanna watched him finish off the rest of the soda and crush the can. Her heart was beating double time. She had no right to ask any questions about his private life, she knew that, but she hadn't been able to control herself. "Sorry," she said, blotting her lips with a paper napkin.

"Hey, no problem," he said.

"I shouldn't be asking you all these questions. It's really none of my business."

"It was no big deal, Johanna. And you can ask me anything. Anything at all." Their eyes met. "Okay?"

Johanna nodded. "Okay."

She smiled. He did, too.

This is going to take a while, he thought.

"Are you really all right?" he asked softly. "I know it's been over a year, but you were in pretty bad shape after the accident."

Johanna crumpled the napkin in her hand. "Yes, I'm fine."

"Did they ever catch the other guy?" Michael asked.

"Who...?"

"The one who caused the accident. The drunk driver."

Johanna straightened. She didn't want to talk about the accident. "No," she said with a shake of her head. "They never did."

"I'm sorry I never made it back to California after the funeral. I know I said I would, but—"

"Don't apologize, Michael. I know how busy you are."

"Yeah. Busy. Well, as long as you're okay."

"I'm okay."

"Good."

Johanna reached out, but stopped short of touching his arm. "Thank you, Michael," she said. "For everything...."

"You don't have to thank me."

As the words were spoken, Michael moved back slightly, his body language making it clear he had no wish to indulge in her expressions of gratitude. She obliged him, quietly sipping her soda as he turned and began rummaging through the kitchen cabinets.

"How do you feel about pasta?" he asked over his shoulder.

"I love it."

"Great. Pasta, I can do," he said, and proceeded to fill one of the copper pots with water.

"Let me," Johanna said as she nudged him away from the sink.

"Uh-uh. For today, you're a guest."

"Only for today?"

"Yep. Tomorrow you go to work," he teased as he set the pot to boil.

Johanna sat on a wooden stool. She felt herself begin to relax as she watched him cook dinner. They made small talk—about the trip, the weather, his parents' upcoming cruise in the Caribbean. It was harmless talk, safe talk.

When the meal was ready, they sat across from each other at the counter and ate in silence. Michael smiled between mouthfuls, and, to be polite, Johanna did the same. It wasn't exactly awkward, yet the comfort level left something to be desired.

It was only natural, Michael told himself. They hadn't really had any kind of defined relationship in a very long time. In many ways, she was a stranger to him, and he was sure she felt the same about him. The questions about his personal life hadn't bothered him nearly as much as they had her. He wondered about that. Johanna, in all the years she'd been married to his brother, had never asked questions such as those tonight.

"We don't know each other very well anymore, do we Johanna?" he said, his thoughts taking life and form.

Johanna looked up at him. She put down her fork. "I suppose not, Michael. I don't remember the last time we had a real conversation."

He did. One summer night many years ago. They'd talked about everything that meant anything to them....

"Let's make a pact," he said. "If either one of us has a question, no matter how silly it may seem, we'll ask away. Will that make you more comfortable with this?"

"I'm not uncomfortable, Michael."

He gave a slight shake to his head. "Yes, you are. So am I—a bit, anyway. Let's give it a try. We'll get to know one another again. How's that sound?"

She shrugged, but her heart was thumping. She didn't want any part of this pact. *Ask me no questions, I'll tell you no lies.*

"Great," she said. She picked up her fork and began eating again. "Just great."

They cleaned up together, and afterward, Michael served a bottle of Chardonnay. It was getting late, and the orange glow of the sun glistened through the branches of the trees.

Johanna stood at the French doors, sipping her wine from a fine crystal goblet as she admired the view of the Watchung Mountains. "I'd almost forgotten how beautifully tranquil the mountains can be here."

Michael kept his distance, leaning against the counter as he watched her. "I would think you'd be used to mountains, living out west all this time."

"It wasn't the same."

"Why not?"

Johanna shrugged. "Oh, I don't know. I guess it just wasn't home."

"Then why did you stay?"

"Jeff wouldn't leave."

He had no answer to that. The words, like the man himself, hung between them.

Michael came up behind her, but Johanna didn't turn. Instead, she caressed the rim of the glass with the tip of her finger. He was so close, she could feel his breath on her neck. For the longest moment, she thought he was going to touch her.

It was something he rarely, if ever, did. In all the years she'd known him, Johanna could count on one hand the number of times they'd come into casual physical contact. It was as if he were reluctant to put his hands on her for any reason.

Even now, he hesitated as if he dared not come any closer. Then slowly, ever so gently, he brushed the backs of his knuckles against her hair. She felt a jolt down to her toes.

She turned to him. His steel blue eyes were bright, almost luminous, as they stared back at her.

Michael touched his glass to hers in a toast. "To Johanna," he said with the barest of smiles. "Welcome home."

Two

He hesitated before knocking on his bedroom door, and when he opened it, Michael knew why.

"Come on in. I'm unpacking."

Johanna was standing by his bed, one knee resting on the edge as she pulled items out of her duffel bag. She was wearing a white V-neck T-shirt, and from what he could tell, little else. He followed the long lines of her legs with his eyes until they were interrupted by the hem of the shirt.

"Something wrong?"

He was staring. "Uh, no," he said, moving deeper into the room. "I need to get my clothes for the morning. I'll be gone before you wake up. I don't want to disturb you."

"Oh, Michael. This is such a beautiful room. I feel awful putting you out of your own bed."

"No problem."

"You should let me sleep on the floor."

"Don't be ridiculous," he said as he disappeared into the walk-in closet.

"No, I'm serious," she called after him. "I'm used to sleeping wherever I fall. The band would sometimes jam until the wee small hours of the morning. If I wanted to sleep, I had to just do it."

Michael returned with his suit, shirt and tie draped over his arm. The little reminder of her erratic life with Jeff only cemented his determination to give up his room. He also caught her suppressing a yawn.

"You're exhausted," he said, "and you've been traveling all day. Get some rest. I'll arrange to have the bedroom set delivered tomorrow. One night on the floor won't kill me."

"Are you sure?"

"I'm sure."

"I guess I am tired," she said as she stretched.

The hem of the T-shirt rose as her arms extended over her head. Michael averted his eyes, but not before he caught a tempting glimpse of her rounded hip.

He swallowed. "Go on to bed, Johanna."

"I think I will," she said, dragging the half-open duffel bag off the bed and onto the floor. She smiled at him, then whipped back the comforter before climbing in. "This is heavenly," she said as she snuggled down.

Michael was singularly moved by the sight of her. Again, the old image of innocence and vulnerability came back to him. She looked like a little girl lost in the big space of her parents' bed. He caught her smiling at him, and their eyes met across the room. He had the urge to go to her, tuck her in, perhaps even brush his lips against her forehead in a comforting good-night kiss.

He looked away and turned to the door.

Who was he kidding? He wanted more than just to comfort her. He *wanted* her, period. His body stirred, and he had to physically stop himself from acting on his inclination and reaching out to her.

He reached for the light switch instead.

"Good night, Michael," she said on a sigh, her voice whisper-soft and, if he didn't know better, inviting.

He flipped the switch. Moonlight from the skylights bathed the room. "Good night, Johanna. Sleep well."

He shut the door behind him, forcing his feet to move one in front of the other until he was down the hall, away from her, in the guest room with the door closed.

Safe.

Michael rested his back against the door and exhaled a breath he hadn't known he'd been holding.

Lord help him, how could he have forgotten the way she affected him?

He'd thought he was over all that. Johanna and Jeff had been married close to ten years, and he had moved on with his life. He was happy, successful and content in both his business and social life.

The days of longing for Johanna were left behind somewhere in the distant past. After the accident, Michael had discovered that Jeff had left her without money or insurance of any kind. It had seemed the most natural thing in the world to want to help, particularly since he'd always felt at least partly responsible for her hasty marriage.

But it was Jeff's vagabond life that really became a bone of contention between them. It had been another one of those things he and Jeff couldn't come to terms with. He'd never approved of Jeff dragging her all around the country, chasing his elusive dream of becoming a major rock star.

It soon became clear to everyone but Jeff that he had neither the talent nor the drive to attain his goal. Yet Jeff held on as tenaciously to his dream as he did to the ever-loyal Johanna, as if somehow the two were inexorably linked. Driven by his fears—of success or failure, Michael was never able to ascertain—Jeff plodded along year after year, town after town, gig after gig.

In the process Johanna had missed out on so much—college, for one thing, not to mention any semblance of a normal life or the prospect of children. The fact that they'd had none surprised no one; Jeff had still been too much of a child himself.

But that was then. They were friends now, and since her parents were now gone, too, Michael and his parents were her only relatives, if only technically. And she trusted him. What was past was past. Johanna had never mentioned the night they'd been together—not once. Neither had he. And he was sure that Jeff never knew. It was almost as if it had never happened.

But it *had* happened, and of all things, he should have remembered what came after....

The craving.

It began the summer night of their neighborhood block party, but it had taken many years and many women for him to make the connection between that night and the constant hollow ache he carried inside.

Michael pushed off the door, shrugged out of his black silk robe and plopped down onto the air mattress on the floor. Lying on his back, he crossed his arms beneath his head and stared at the ceiling, purposely doing something he'd promised himself he'd never do again.

Remembering . . .

She'd been seventeen, sweet, innocent and—as was always the case—all over him. He'd been flattered by her attention, but until that night, hadn't taken her very seriously.

The entire neighborhood was at the block party that Fourth of July, and by midnight, it was still going strong. Somehow, he and Johanna had ended up at his house. One thing had led to another, and soon they were in each other's arms.

They'd made love—he, only marginally more experienced than she, yet at the time he would have vigorously denied the truth of that.

It had been magical, unreal, as perfect as a first-time fantasy could ever be. They'd had what some people called chemistry, that certain *something* that enables two people to melt into one another, to truly become one.

It had not been in his realm of experience to know that then, and by the time he did realize what they'd had together, it was too late.

For later that same night his brother, in one of those rare coincidences that sometimes change lives, made a confession to Michael about his feelings for Johanna. Without hesitation, the next day Michael had put an end to whatever had started the night before. It had been the least he could do for his brother—for Jeff, who had always felt so inferior, who was always playing catch-up to Michael's successes. Stepping aside seemed not only the right thing to do, it had been the only thing to do.

Michael had known he'd hurt her, but he hadn't realized how much until two months later when his parents called him at college and told him that Jeff and Johanna had eloped.

He'd been stunned by the news. After that, they saw each other only rarely. Though Michael was sure that Jeff never knew about him and Johanna, there had been enough rivalry between the brothers to make visiting a trial rather than a pleasure.

And whether he liked to admit it or not, Michael had been jealous. Jealous of what his brother had. His brother's wife. It hadn't been easy living with the knowledge that he'd once had her in the palm of his hand, and then pushed her—no, *given*—her away.

He'd made the supreme sacrifice for his brother. It had seemed so clear at the time, so noble. Yet as the years had passed, his grand gesture offered cold comfort on long winter nights. For no one had ever made him feel the way he'd felt with Johanna that summer night . . . and the ache never really went away.

Which made Johanna all the more dangerous now. For if his brother's wife had been out of reach, his brother's widow was completely taboo. He had offered to help her, protect her, not be the cause of more trouble. She'd been through enough, and she didn't need the added problem of her brother-in-law panting after her.

He shut his eyes and tried to rest. He had a busy day tomorrow, starting with an early morning meeting with a potential client for which he had to be sharp. Try as he might, though, sleep was elusive, and he had the distinct feeling that with Johanna down the hall, tonight was only the first of many restless nights to come.

By late afternoon the next day the new bedroom furniture had arrived. Johanna waited for the delivery men to set it up, then proceeded to make the bed with the new sheets and spread Michael had stored in the closet.

She stood back to admire her work. The Victorian tearose linens were very feminine and pretty. The room looked cozy and comfortable, and she was pleased that Michael had gone to so much trouble to make her feel at home.

Johanna returned to Michael's bedroom to pick up her belongings. She paused by the door on her way out. Light spilled in from all directions, the rays of the sun crisscrossing at odd angles, filling each nook and cranny with a glowing warmth. She felt drawn to it, wishing she could dip her hands into the light and splash it on her face like warm water. It was so peaceful, and she lingered a minute to admire the sight.

She had meant what she said. This was a beautiful room. Truly a master suite. She'd loved sleeping in Michael's big bed last night, felt as if she belonged there. Her arms and legs had reached as far as they could without running out of space, without touching anything... or anyone.

Michael.

For one very brief moment last night, she thought he was going to come to her. He didn't, of course, but the moment was there, and she'd felt it down to her toes.

She wanted him to, wanted him to come to her, touch her, if only as a friend, if only in welcome.

She hungered for it. It had been so very long since she'd been touched by anyone at all.

Johanna made her way back to her own room at the other end of the hallway. It seemed a long walk, as if Michael had picked the farthest place to put her, as if he were afraid she'd pester him, start throwing herself at him again, the way she used to when they were young.

She unpacked the duffel bag haphazardly, shutting her eyes for a moment in renewed mortification at the memory of her adolescent behavior.

Especially that night.

Lord, she'd practically *forced* him to make love with her! But she had been so in love that she couldn't see or feel anything but him—his hands, his lips, his body on hers. It had been wonderful, everything she'd ever dreamed making love should be.

Until the next morning when he'd knocked on her door bright and early to apologize for taking advantage of her. She was too young, he'd said, and he had to finish college. It was a mistake, he'd said, and she'd agreed, very maturely and wholeheartedly nodding to each sentence he uttered while her heart was breaking into a million tiny pieces inside her chest.

Jeff had picked up those pieces. He had been right there, and it had been too easy to let him. It had been a long time before anything mattered after that. By then, she'd been married to a man she cared for but didn't love, yet she had been committed to try to make it work. It hadn't been Jeff's fault, only hers, and she had made every effort possible to insure that Jeff never suffered. She had grown up real fast, putting those adolescent dreams behind her, knowing better than anyone that she and Michael could never be.

Storing the duffel bag in the closet, she made her way down to the kitchen for a cup of tea. Well, she'd learned her lesson. She would never do that to herself, let alone Michael, ever again. He was helping her out of a tough spot, as much for Jeff's memory as for herself. She appreciated it, but she wasn't for a minute going to make him feel more responsible for her than he already did.

She may have been his brother's wife, but she wasn't going to become his burden. Not Michael's. She couldn't bear it.

"Hi."

Johanna looked up. "Oh, I didn't hear you come in."

"You were lost in thought."

"You're early. You said six."

Michael placed his briefcase on the counter. "I know. I wanted to see if the furniture arrived. Did it?"

"Yes, it's lovely."

"Then you like the room?"

"Very much." She smiled. "Of course, you spoiled me last night with all that space. I'm going to miss sleeping in your bed...."

Michael felt the blood rush through his body as her words formed a picture in his mind. Johanna in his bed. Like last night, only better. He was next to her ... His body stirred, but his face turned to stone. He had to stop this, and soon. Johanna had no idea what she'd said. She was an innocent, and he was an oversexed cad.

He tried to smile and make light of it, but he couldn't manage to get the corners of his mouth to turn up. Instead, their eyes met.

Johanna felt her face turn red as his blue eyes pinned her and her words echoed back. How could she have *said* such a thing? She had just finished admonishing herself not to put him in an awkward position, and here she was talking about his *bed!* He was evidently embarrassed. Lord, what was wrong with her?

She turned away from him, wishing she had saved that last cigarette instead of throwing it away. She needed to get away, if only for a while.

"I was sitting here thinking about taking a ride," she said, reaching for the key rack. "Is it okay?" she asked, dangling the keys to the Jeep toward Michael.

"Of course," he said, "I told you that the Jeep was for you to use anytime. "Where are you going?"

"Shopping," Johanna said.

"For what?"

"I thought I'd go to the mall and look at some clothes. I'll need them for school and the office—"

"And dinner parties," Michael added.

"Oh?"

"I have a client I'm trying to woo. Can you cook, Johanna?"

"Adequately."

"Then great. We can plan something if I sign him."

"Sure."

"Maybe I can help. Mind if I come along?"

"No, of course not," she said, wondering how she'd suddenly lost control of her escape.

Johanna drove the Jeep with Michael giving her instructions. The roads had changed little since she'd lived in the area, but somehow it all looked different. Strange. Or perhaps it was only she who was the stranger. She glanced at Michael. He was looking out the passenger window, not paying much attention to her or her driving. Again, she wished for a cigarette.

He turned to her, and she managed a tight smile.

"Hey," he said, covering her hand with his own. "You're gripping that wheel like it's a life preserver. What's wrong, Johanna?"

"Nothing really. Except I don't remember the roads the way I used to."

"Understandable," he said, "It's been almost ten years since you've lived here."

He pulled his hand away, not because he wanted to but because he couldn't think of a good reason not to.

"I can't remember the last time I shopped here," she said as she pulled into the Short Hills Mall parking lot. "Maybe my prom dress," she added, cutting the engine.

"A long time ago," he said.

Johanna laughed at his solemnity. "Yes. A very long time ago!"

Their eyes met again, and this time all of the warmth and none of the baggage of their history passed between them. They shared a slow smile.

"Let's go," he said.

Johanna picked the first department store they happened upon. She wasn't much of a shopper, having had neither the time nor the money in recent years to build a wardrobe. Not that she'd needed it, living Jeff's life-style. T-shirts and jeans served just about any purpose.

But for Michael, she needed more. If she was going to work for him, hostess for him, she would need *real* clothes.

"You take this rack, I'll take that one," Michael said as he pointed to the dress department.

Efficient as ever, Johanna thought, as she nodded and complied. It was amazing how different the brothers were. Jeff couldn't have cared less about what she wore, or what they did, or where they went. She had made all the decisions in the marriage, in many ways acting more like his mother than his wife. She grinned to herself at Michael's authoritative manner. While she had no desire to be led around by the nose, it was nice to have someone else take the lead for a change.

"Size?" he asked.

"Eight. I think. At least, that was my size the last time I bought something like this."

They rummaged through the racks back-to-back. Michael was the first to find something. He held it up for her inspection.

"How about this?"

Johanna gave the dress the once-over. It was a pretty but busy floral print with a white bib collar trimmed with lace. It was also high-necked and mid-calf length with a row of delicate buttons down the front.

"Pretty," she said.

"But you don't like it?"

"No."

"Okay."

Michael put the dress back on the rack and continued to look. "How about this?"

She turned to him again and made a face.

"What's wrong with it?"

"Frumpy."

"Frumpy?"

"Yes," she said, "Look at it. It has a high neck, long sleeves, and the length is almost down to the ankle."

"Winter's coming. It'll keep you warm."

Johanna laughed. "That's for sure!" Finding something she did like, she held it out for his inspection. "Now, this is more like it."

Michael grimaced. The dress was short, a classic black knit with a scooped neck and long, tapered sleeves. It would hug her body like a glove.

"Isn't that a bit too extreme?"

"No, I don't think so," she said as she hung the dress over her arm to try on later.

After picking out several other outfits, all under Michael's disapproving gaze, Johanna entered the fitting room. Her favorite was the black knit, and she trotted out to show him how it looked.

"What do you think?" she asked.

All Michael's fears reached fruition as Johanna strutted in front of the mirror. She looked fantastic, as if she'd been melted down and poured into the dress. Every curve of her body was visible, accentuated—her round, high breasts, her hips, her tight, lush bottom. It was exactly the type of dress he'd have picked out for a woman he was dating, a woman he wanted to show off... a woman he wanted to bed.

"It's too short," he said. "And too tight."

"No, it's not," Johanna said as she admired herself. "I think it looks great. As if it was made for me."

"As if it was *painted* on you, you mean."

She smiled indulgently. "Oh, Michael, you're such a stuffed shirt."

"Johanna—"

"Don't you like it?"

"I like it fine. It's just—"

"Don't you think your client will like it?"

"I'm sure he will, but that's not the point."

She leaned toward him. "Then what is?"

She was standing close to him. Too close. Her scent swirled around him. Intoxicating. He shut his eyes. And with that came control. "If you want the dress that badly, get it."

Johanna grinned. "I intend to." She reentered the dressing room and changed back into her jeans. He made a face when she handed the saleswoman the dress and said, "I'll take it."

They split up after that. Michael had the distinct feeling that he would be better off if he didn't have to watch her try on any more clothes. Each time she modeled something, his mind registered, then catalogued, every move, which he knew would only be dredged up in the wee hours of the morning while he was trying to sleep. After setting a time and place to meet, he went off on his own with the weak excuse that he needed some shirts.

Johanna watched him walk off in what seemed to be a huff. She hadn't meant to be defiant about the knit dress, so to appease him she purchased two relatively conservative skirts and blouses and a navy blue blazer. That was about all her beleaguered charge account could handle, so she made her way to the escalator where she and Michael planned to meet.

She arrived first, and while she was waiting, her peripheral vision caught sight of a royal blue negligee hanging on display at the edge of the lingerie department. Checking to see that Michael was nowhere around, she sought out the gown and held it up for inspection.

Its diaphanous material was all but transparent, except for some strategically placed satin appliqués. It was, without a doubt, the most flagrantly female thing she had ever laid her eyes on, let alone owned.

Reverently, Johanna touched the satin water lilies with the tips of her fingers. She felt a twinge inside as she checked the price tag. Way out of her range. Her practical side told her no, but the woman in her wouldn't let her walk away. A little red-horned devil seemed to be sitting on her shoulder, taunting her, tempting her to throw caution to the wind and buy it.

Not that she had any reason to wear it—or anyone to wear it for—but still, she couldn't deny she wanted it, if for no other reason than it was so beautiful.

She felt Michael come up behind her. "It's fabulous, isn't it?" she asked.

It was damn sexy to him, but he said, "Yes."

A salesperson moved into her line of vision. "Can I ring that up for you?" she asked.

"Oh, no," Johanna said as she caressed the material longingly. "I was just admiring it." She turned and began to walk back toward the escalator.

"Why didn't you get it if you liked it that much?" Michael asked.

"Didn't you see the price tag? I couldn't justify buying it."

Michael stood still for a moment before following her to the escalator, the look on her face as she touched the material of the nightgown fresh in his mind. He pulled her arm before she got on. "Let me get it for you."

"Oh, Michael, no."

"Why not?"

"I really don't need it."

"But you *want* it. And I want to get it for you."

"Michael . . ."

He touched her cheek with the back of his hand. "I can buy a gift for you, can't I?"

"Of course—"

"Then . . ." he extended his arm, escorting her back into the lingerie department.

The salesperson was waiting for them. "Changed your mind?" she asked.

"Yes," Johanna said with a side glance to Michael. "I suppose I have."

The woman picked out the negligee, checked for the correct size and led the way to the register. "This is beautiful, isn't it?" she said to Johanna. "Your husband is very generous."

"Oh, he's not my husband," Johanna said with a laugh. "He's my . . ."

Just then Michael's eyes met hers. Something passed between them, something electric, white-hot and sizzling. Something potent, portentous.

A look.

A wish.

A promise.

The salesperson coughed, and both of them returned their attention to her. Michael handed her his credit card.

"You know," the woman said as she folded the nightgown in tissue, "there is a darling matching robe that goes with it. May I show it to you?"

"No—"

"Yes—"

The salesperson smiled. "I'll be right back."

While she was gone, Johanna turned to Michael. "Michael, this is insane. You've already spent a fortune on this. I don't need the robe, too!"

"Here it is," the woman said, returning with a robe matching the negligee in color. It, though, was not transparent. It would cover her up from neck to toes.

That did it. "We'll take it," Michael said.

"I don't need both," Johanna whispered to him as the salesperson rang up the sale and packed the items away in a shopping bag.

Michael took hold of the bag with one hand and Johanna's elbow with the other as he led her toward the escalator.

"The nightgown is for you." He stopped before stepping on. His gaze met hers. "The robe, Johanna, is for *me*."

Three

——

Johanna spent most of the next two weeks analyzing Michael's comment about the robe. It wasn't in his nature to make that kind of remark. He didn't joke—at least, not like that; his humor was more subtle and wry. So she was more than curious about what he meant by it.

But *was* he just kidding, teasing her the way he had when she was a girl? Or was this the serious, practical, conservative Michael speaking, subtly letting her know that he wanted her to keep covered up, out of his sight?

Or—and she was sure this wasn't it—was he actually *bothered* by the thought of her parading around the house in that flimsy nightgown?

As if she would ever do that!

The nightgown and robe were safely hanging in the back of her closet. Somehow she didn't see herself wearing the nightgown to bed any old night. It had to be a special occasion of some sort, but she hadn't a clue *what* sort. It was a frivolous gift, useless really, but still, she liked the idea of owning it, liked it even better that Michael had bought it for her. She harbored a secret desire to model it for him, the way she'd modeled the black knit dress. How would he react? Like Michael, her brother-in-law, or Michael, the man?

Johanna checked the clock and then the roast in the oven. Still lost in thought, she ambled around the kitchen table, setting it for dinner.

It was the man she wanted. Had always wanted. Somehow the brother-in-law thing had gotten in the way. Though she knew he didn't feel the same way about her, Johanna couldn't help but fantasize about him. He had always been her ideal—his chiseled good looks and his strong, silent manner tugged at her still.

It seemed as if all those young-girl dreams were coming back with a force she couldn't control—especially now, living in his home, doing his laundry, cooking his meals. It was almost like playing house. They seemed like two children immersed in some sort of game that was all show, no substance.

Johanna wanted the substance.

Opening the oven, she pierced the baked potato with a fork to test it. Dinner was close to ready, and she expected Michael to come walking through the door momentarily. She'd had a busy day, but wasn't a bit tired. The first thing in the morning, she had registered at a local college, arranging to take two classes, one day and one evening.

She was excited by the prospect of becoming a student again and couldn't wait to tell Michael about it. She truly felt as if she were embarking on a new life. There was so much she wanted to learn, do, be . . . and most of all, share. But the one she wanted to share it with didn't reciprocate the feeling.

Oh, sure, Michael offered her friendship, support—financial and otherwise—but when she'd come back from registration today, she had wanted to jump for joy. She wanted to hug and be hugged, touch and be touched on the most basic of human levels. When Michael came through that door tonight, though he'd be happy for her, he wouldn't satisfy those needs. He'd kept her at arm's length all her life, and she had no reason to believe that would change.

So with the want came a need, and that, too, couldn't be fulfilled. It tempered the happiness of the day, created a void in her soul—a void she felt had been there all her life.

Sometimes she wondered if what she was looking for was even attainable. She'd been married to Jeff, and though it had been a chaotic relationship in some ways, she never really doubted that Jeff loved her. In the beginning of the marriage, he had even been very attentive, but still she had felt as if she were only going through the motions of what marriage should be. No matter how hard she tried to make it work, she never felt truly satisfied.

What was wrong with her? Why hadn't it been enough?

The marriage had been over and done with long before Jeff's accident, though no one knew it. They'd developed a relationship more like brother and sister than husband and wife. In the latter years of her marriage, she'd handled not only his band's bookings, but all the little details of his life, as well. It wasn't exactly what she'd wanted to do with her life, but it had kept her busy. She'd brought up the subject of separating many times, but Jeff always fought it.

She'd stayed with him because of guilt, because she knew he was afraid that he'd be lost without her, because she'd felt she had nowhere to go, and because he begged her to, even when they'd stopped sleeping together...even that last year after he'd found someone new.

Strange as it seemed, she hadn't been the least bit jealous. In fact, she had been happy for Jeff, and hoped that the new relationship would work for him, would give him what he needed . . . would set her free.

It was what she'd told him the night of the accident, but he'd been frightened by the idea of her leaving. He had come to depend on her too much, and had almost a child's temper tantrum when she told him it was over. He'd stormed out, into the night, into the rain, too angry, too hurt...and in no condition to drive.

The accident had been horrible, abruptly and unforgivingly putting an end to life as she knew it. She'd felt lost, adrift for the longest time, and guilty still for not taking better care of Jeff, for not telling the whole truth to his family. It wasn't that she'd lied exactly, she'd just chosen to leave out certain details of the accident she knew would upset them. And what was the point? Jeff was dead. Better a sin of omission to spare their feelings than an unsatisfactory explanation from her about what had happened that night.

She opened the oven door and checked the meat thermometer before resetting the timer.

She wondered how Michael would feel if he knew about her part in Jeff's accident. Though they'd had their differences, the brothers had a strong and abiding love for each other. Michael's sense of fairness and his loyalty were just two of the reasons why she was here today. Would he look so kindly on her if he knew the truth?

"Mmm . . . what smells so good?"

Johanna looked up. Michael stood by the kitchen entrance, casually leaning against the doorjamb. He held his briefcase in one hand and dangled his jacket over his shoulder with the other. He had a classic thank-God-it's-Friday expression on his face, and though his tie was still perfectly knotted and his shirt still neatly starched, he looked about as relaxed as she'd ever seen him.

She returned her attention to preparing dinner, fighting a desire to loosen his tie, open his top shirt button and kiss him hello. "I thought this would be a good night for a roast," she said.

The weather had turned cool with a foreshadowing of autumn in the air. When she'd stepped out the door that morning, she'd felt the chill down to her bones and had run back in for a bulky turtleneck sweater. For Johanna, who was more accustomed to sunny California, the change was drastic.

Michael laughed. He dropped his briefcase and jacket on a chair and moved next to her. "You'll have to get your winter skin back," he said, giving the back of her sweater a playful tug as he leaned over the counter. "What are you going to cook when the temperature dips below thirty?"

"Chicken soup and hot chocolate," she said with a grin, then shooed him away as he opened the oven door to check the roast. "*And* we'll light a fire."

Michael's eyes glazed over at the thought. Johanna in winter. Snow outside, a fire blazing inside. "I think I'll look forward to that," he said softly as he leaned against the counter.

Johanna studied him. His blue eyes were off somewhere else, dreamy, and she wondered what picture had formed in his mind. She looked away. It was probably something innocuous, like the need to chop wood or something practical like that. He wouldn't be thinking as she was of the two of them lying side by side on the rug, basking in the glow of the fire.

"Dinner will be ready soon," she said.

Michael reluctantly pushed himself off the counter, returning to the here and now. "About how long?"

"A half hour or so."

He rubbed the back of his neck. "I'm tight as a coil," he said. "I think I'll go down and work out for a while."

"Fine," Johanna said. "I'll call you when it's ready."

Michael ran upstairs, quickly changed into shorts and a sweatshirt and headed for the basement and his workout equipment. He adjusted the weights and laid back on the bench to begin pressing.

One thing he could say for Johanna, since she'd arrived, he'd been diligent in his exercise program. His muscles protested as he pushed himself harder. If nothing else, his body would benefit from his growing frustration. Working at the office all day and working out each evening had made him exhausted enough to fall into his bed at night and sleep...as opposed to lying wide-awake on his back, staring at the stars through the skylight while thinking about ways to stop thinking about Johanna.

About what he wanted to do to her, with her.

He increased the weights.

Beads of perspiration broke out first on his chest, then his forehead, as he continued to pump. He changed positions and began working his legs and abdomen, attempting—if not succeeding—to lose himself in the sheer physicality of his actions.

But while the exercise helped, it didn't cure the problem. Because there was only one cure for what was ailing him, and she was upstairs right now in the kitchen making nice to a roast.

The picture warmed him even more than the exercise. Right or wrong, he loved coming home to find her there, in his kitchen, in his life. It was old-fashioned and probably downright chauvinistic, but the thought of her waiting for him at the end of a hectic day provided a bright spot, an anchor for him as he worked.

At odd times, an image of her in one particular room or another would form in his mind, and a wave of satisfaction would wash over him. It amazed him that he felt this way, having never been a particular fan of the joys of domesticity. Without conceit, he'd had many an opportunity over the years to make a commitment, to move a relationship that single vital step forward into something more...into marriage.

Yet he had never had the remotest desire to do so.

He'd told himself that no woman had inspired him to change his life so dramatically. He was set in his ways, comfortable with himself and his life-style. But he was beginning to believe that the fault rested squarely on his shoulders. He'd used his career and his business as an excuse to keep that kind of commitment at arm's length. The fact that the times he felt something lacking were few and far between had been enough to convince him that he was right—some people just weren't cut out for hearth, home and family.

But with Johanna here, he had a taste of what he'd been missing. Living with someone was not the chore he'd thought it would be. She didn't interfere with him in the least; in fact, she enhanced every aspect of his home life.

He *liked* coming down to find a hot breakfast instead of just gulping down a cold cup of overbrewed coffee from the convenience store on his way to work. She'd insisted on rising with him each morning and sending him off even after he'd told her there was no need. But he had to admit that sitting across the table from her sleepy face was nothing short of pure pleasure, a tonic to jump-start his day, and something to which he was quickly becoming addicted.

He wondered how he'd managed to function without her. In such a short time she had weaved herself so thoroughly into the fabric of his life.

It was great. It was fun. He enjoyed it. And yet he wanted more. So much more.

"Want a taste?"

Michael stopped pumping and turned his head in the direction of her voice. Johanna stood a few steps away, holding a small plate in one hand and a forkful of roast beef in the other.

"Sure," he said.

He sat up as she approached. His breath was short, and his heart was beating double time as Johanna lifted the fork to his mouth. Her hand began to shake, and Michael looked into her eyes before reaching up to steady her by holding her wrist. With his teeth, he pulled the piece of meat into his mouth and chewed.

"Delicious."

Johanna's heart was pounding. She shouldn't have come down here, she knew that. She should have waited for him to come up on his own or called him from the top of the stairs. But she hadn't been able to help herself. As always, Michael drew her to him like a sliver of wire to a strong magnet. She wanted to see him, be in the same room with him. But seeing him in this state, without the social trappings and security of a suit, shirt and tie, was a mistake of the worst kind. This self-inflicted torture was only feeding a fantasy that had no basis in reality.

Oozing masculinity, he looked and smelled like a man, sweat glistening on his forehead, arms and legs, an oval blotch darkening the middle of his gray sweatshirt. The heat of his body radiated out to her, and she felt a tiny throbbing deep inside respond with a corresponding heat of her own. She'd never been as closely aware of him as she was at this moment. Her knees became weak, and she wet her lips with her tongue.

"Is it cooked enough?"

He took the fork and plate out of her hands and finished the last piece. "It is for me."

Johanna picked a white towel off a rack to blot his brow. "You're all sweaty," she said.

He made no move to stop her as she wiped his face and arms. Though he knew he should, it felt too good.

"I should shower," he said when she finished. They exchanged the fork and dish for the towel. He wiped his hands and hung the towel around his neck.

"Yes," Johanna said, but didn't move away from his side.

"Do I have time?" Michael clenched his fists and rested them on his knees so as not to grab her by the waist and pull her between his legs. He wanted to hug her to him, knead her soft, round buttocks in the palms of his hands and bury his face in the space between her breasts.

Please go away, Johanna.

"I can keep it warm," she said.

And still she didn't move away.

He tried to rise from the bench without touching her, but she was too close, and he couldn't manage it. They bumped, and Michael reached out to steady her. He held her by her arms, unconsciously caressing the soft skin in the crease of her elbows with his thumbs.

The moment hung in the air as their eyes met. They were close, so close they could hear each other breathing.

Johanna was frozen to the spot, anticipating his next move, almost willing him to make it. She wanted him to kiss her, begged him with her eyes to do it, but as she felt his body lean forward, panic set in. What was she doing? What would happen to her if he did? How would she handle it... afterward?

Overcome with her own questions and fears, Johanna lowered her head, breaking eye contact.

Michael dropped his hands and stepped back. "I'll be quick," he said.

She nodded, unable to speak, unable to move. The fork and dish were held rigidly in her hands, serving no one, no purpose, as she stood alone in the exercise room, listening to his footsteps fade on the steps behind her.

She stood there for a long time, long enough to hear the water run through the pipes as he turned on the shower upstairs. The sound galvanized her into action, and she turned to the stairway, climbing slowly back to the kitchen and the safety of her fantasy world.

Michael rested his palms against the shower tiles and let the hot water pelt his aching muscles. His body was taut, hard, and he had an erection of the worst kind—with no hope of relief. He breathed deeply, trying to dispel the sight and feel of her, trying to get himself back in control.

What a fool! He had actually been about to kiss her. All she had to do was wipe his forehead with a towel, and whatever vestiges of control with which he'd prided himself had flown out the window. He'd even deluded himself into imagining he'd seen an invitation in her eyes, instead of only Johanna's innocent and innate kindness.

He turned the water to cold and screamed his frustration into the stream that ran down his face and body, inflicting a vengeful reality. Abruptly, he turned off the faucet and stood for a moment, naked and dripping, miserably under control and determined to stay that way.

Get a grip, he told himself.

He would not embarrass her or himself again.

He dressed in clean jeans and a V-neck teal blue golf sweater before heading for the kitchen. When he arrived, the roast was sitting on a serving platter, sliced and decorated with sprigs of parsley. His mouth began to water, not just

from the sight and smell of the food, but from the sight and
smell of Johanna as she puttered at the sink.

The craving returned in full force as he watched her, his
only notion to walk up behind her, reach around and cup
her full breasts in his hands. He'd press himself into her, and
she would fit so perfectly against him, he knew she would,
as if God had made her especially for him....

He shut his eyes against the pain his futile thoughts
brought. But the image remained.

How could this seem so right, feel so good...and be so
impossible?

"Just in time," she said, acknowledging his presence.

He tried to smile back, but couldn't, his determination
altering his features.

Johanna noted the back-to-business look immediately. It
was the one he used whenever she was getting too friendly,
too intimate. There was an implicit warning in that look. It
said in no uncertain terms, *Don't get too close, Johanna.
Remember what happened the last time.* He was giving her
fair warning that whatever intimacy she might imagine was
present in this arrangement was definitely one-sided.

It was strange how tuned in to him she was, as if she could
read his body language, tell by the look in his eyes or the ri-
gidity of his spine if he was happy or sad, excited or bored,
calm or anxious.

What he was now was cautious, and she had no doubt
that her behavior downstairs earlier was the reason.

She took her place across from him at the table and began to eat dinner.

"Bad day?" she asked.

"No. Not really. Just very busy."

"How's the project going?" she asked.

"Slowly but surely. We have a month before our turn to make the presentation. We've got some stiff competition, though."

"This sounds as if it's very important to you."

"It is," he said between mouthfuls. "Landing the Larsen account will mean the difference between a good year and a great one for my people."

"I wish you luck," she said conversationally.

"We'll need more than luck. Jack Larsen is a tough Texan who knows what he wants. The presentation is going to have to be top-notch. I'd feel a lot better if we weren't so shorthanded." He paused. "Have you given any thought to working part-time at the office as we discussed?"

"No, I haven't. I thought you would want me to help with furnishing the house first."

"That's a priority, too," he said, then pointed to his dish with his fork. "Mmm, this is really excellent, Johanna."

"Thank you. I'm glad you like it."

"I do. Maybe you could make this again if we can arrange to have Larsen and his wife over for dinner."

"Sure," she said. "When will that be?"

"I don't know yet," he said as he pushed his dish away. "As soon as the presentation's ready, I suppose."

They cleaned off the table together. Michael seemed preoccupied with his thoughts as he rinsed off the dishes and placed them in the dishwasher.

"I can come into the office to help next week, if you need me," she offered.

"I do, but I don't want to interfere with your settling in."

"You wouldn't be. We can shop for furniture tomorrow if you have no plans."

"Other than some paperwork, I have no plans at all. It sounds fine to me. We can measure the den tonight and leave first thing after breakfast."

"Okay."

After they finished cleaning up, Michael rummaged through his junk drawer and came up with a tape measure. Johanna held one end and he trailed around with the other as they mapped out the dimensions of the room. They did the same in the dining room and living room, then took a break.

Johanna made hot chocolate, and though it wasn't quite cold enough for a fire, they sat side by side on the floor in front of the fireplace, anyway.

"This is great," Michael said. "I can't remember the last time I had hot chocolate. And with a marshmallow, no less."

"They had a display in the supermarket. I couldn't resist."

"Oh, one of those," he said.

"One of what?"

"An impulse shopper."

Johanna laughed. "Me? Never. There was never enough money for me to be impulsive about *anything*."

Michael's face turned serious. "I'm sorry, Johanna. Jeff was my brother and I loved him, but we never did see eye to eye on his life-style."

"You've nothing to be sorry about, Michael. You've been very generous, and I appreciate it more than I can say. But you aren't responsible for me now any more than you were when Jeff was alive."

He knew she was trying to make him feel better with her remark, but it only served as a reminder that he was nothing to her other than Jeff's brother.

He nodded his tacit agreement, took a sip of hot chocolate and changed the subject. "So what did you do today?"

"I enrolled in school—"

Michael pushed up onto his knees. "Johanna, that's great! Why didn't you say something?"

"I meant to. We . . . I just got sidetracked."

He placed his mug on the black slate fireplace step. "So tell me."

"It's only one day class and one night class to start—"

"What are you taking?"

Her enthusiasm returning with his reaction, Johanna sat up on her knees, too, placing her mug next to his, and faced him. "Well, I thought I'd start out with English and art history."

"I know how much this means to you," he said. "You don't seem too excited—"

"Oh, but I am! The campus is small, but it has everything! I can't wait to start."

"When is that?"

"Week after next."

He took her by the shoulders and turned her to face him. "Johanna . . . I'm so proud of you," he said. And because he felt he should, he added, "Jeff would be, too."

"Yes." Johanna pulled away from him.

"Did I say something wrong?"

She shook her head. "No, of course not."

"Does it upset you to talk about him? Do you still miss him that much?" Michael asked.

She smiled a slow, sad smile. "Not in the way you think."

"In what way, then?"

She sighed, not really wanting to discuss Jeff with him, but knowing that it was inevitable. "I miss . . . this. You know, having someone to talk to, to share things with. . . ."

"That's what I'm here for," he said.

"To take Jeff's place?"

Michael stiffened and his eyes grew hard. "No, I couldn't do that even if I wanted to. Which I don't."

She stared back at him just as intently. "I wouldn't want you to."

Slowly, purposefully, he turned her toward him until their bodies were almost touching. Steel blue eyes scanned warm hazel ones as he studied her face.

"What do you want, Johanna?"

"I don't know, Michael. Truly I don't. Things are moving so fast right now. Good things. Things I've wanted all my life. And all because of you. I'm grateful—"

"I don't want your gratitude."

"I know that, but I wouldn't be able to do all of this if it weren't for you," she said softly.

Michael shook his head. "You're wrong. I have nothing to do with this. It's you. Who you are. Who you've become. You've been through so much, but you refuse to let it stop you. You're beautiful, Johanna, and brave—"

"Not brave. Scared to death."

His fingers caressed her shoulders as he pulled her to him. "Don't be. I'm here for you whenever you need me."

Oh, Michael, if you only knew how much I need you now.

Johanna parted her lips in silent invitation. Michael leaned forward and kissed her. She was in need of comforting, and that was all right. She'd earned it, deserved it, and he had no problem filling the bill. The key was to keep it light, keep it gentle and not let on to her that her scent made his head spin, his heart pound and his body tighten.

A kiss, he repeated to himself, only a friendly, *brotherly* kiss.

But then her arms reached around him, and she pressed herself into him. He broke away from that sweet, tender kiss and looked down at her. Her hazel eyes were bright, rimmed in green, and her face was flushed.

She was asking something of him, something she couldn't put into words, something more than a friendly kiss. But did she mean it?

There was only one way to find out.

Michael put his hands on her waist and pulled her to him. Their knees almost touched as he leaned into her, his face a fraction of an inch away from hers. He gave her time to protest, but she didn't. Instead, she tilted her head expectantly. Slowly, carefully, he brushed his lips against hers, their breath mixing as he coaxed her lips apart.

And then he slanted his head and took her mouth whole. He didn't give himself a chance to think, only act. His tongue swept inside. She tasted hot, chocolaty and marshmallow sweet. In an instant, his body hardened against her.

Johanna's spine stiffened with the impact, then went limp. She reached up and grabbed hold of his shoulders. Michael ran his hands down her back and cupped her bottom, pushing into her at the same time. She felt all of him. Every part of him. A feeling of joy burst through her system.

He was aroused. Very, very aroused.

It was contagious. She felt herself melt from the inside out. With each tug of his mouth, she felt a corresponding pull in the center of her being. She was drawn into a whirlpool of sensation, and for the first time in a very long time, she let herself go and gave herself over to feeling.

Michael couldn't keep still. His hands roamed all over her, returning to her waist, up the curve of her back, around to the undersides of her arms. When his thumbs grazed the outer edges of her breasts, he felt her shudder against him.

That did it. It was as if all bets were off, as if all the admonishments he had given himself in the last two weeks were being replayed to him in unintelligible ancient hieroglyphics. The words of warning were there, swirling around inside his head, but they were not connecting, and the message was jumbled, lost.

Johanna was beyond reason. This was her dream, her fantasy come true. It couldn't be real, she told herself, but his hands were real, his lips were real, and his hard *body* couldn't be more real. She spread her knees and rubbed herself against him like a purring cat.

With that, whatever semblance of coherency Michael had was gone. He fit himself into her perfectly, so perfectly that if they hadn't had any clothes on, he'd have been inside her. The thought shot through him like a jolt of electricity. He was on fire, crazed, out of control . . . out of his mind.

He pulled her down with him onto the rug, ready to make the thought a reality, but in the process, his arm hit the mugs . . . and the cooled chocolate liquid spilled all over them and the rug.

They jumped to their feet, glancing down at the mess and then at each other.

Johanna was dazed, Michael in shock.

He shook his head to clear it. "Excuse me," he said, his voice polite but strained as he left her and went into the kitchen.

He was back before Johanna could bring herself to move. What had happened? The last thing she remembered they were talking about school . . . about Jeff. . . . She was thanking him for his help. . . .

Michael returned with a roll of paper towels. As if in slow motion, she tore off a few, joining him as he cleaned up the spill.

The physical activity was good for her, it helped calm her, if only for the moment. And that was all she needed—one moment to get away from him, to hide in her room, to think about what happened in the privacy of her safe fantasy world.

When the stain was cleaned, Johanna sat back and stared into space for the briefest of moments. She couldn't move very quickly, still dazed, still filled with an unnamed longing.

She turned to look at him. Fire blue eyes stared back at her. She had no idea how she looked. Wild probably, confused definitely. She touched her fingertips to her lips. They were throbbing, and she knew her mouth was swollen.

Michael had to say something, for her sake if not his own. He could tell she was frightened by what had happened. Hell, he was pretty shaken up himself. He was sure she hadn't been expecting anything so passionate from him. What had started as a comforting gesture had turned into something that could pierce her trust for him like an arrow to the heart.

He didn't want that to happen. More than anything, he wanted to take her in his arms and comfort her, tell her everything would be all right, he would protect her. But protecting her from himself would be a hard case to sell....

"I frightened you," he said. "I'm sorry."

"No, I'm the one who should be apologizing. I feel so foolish...like a love-starved widow—"

"Don't..." he said, running a hand around the back of her neck.

He pulled her to him, resting his chin on her head. He was back in control, passion shelved for the time being. Only for the time being. He needed to be alone, away from her to do what Johanna would call his "Michael thing"—to analyze this, to dissect his actions, to discover why he had lost control so quickly and so completely. To make sure it didn't happen again.

Johanna broke away from him. She looked up into his eyes and wondered what he thought about her, not quite sure she really wanted to know.

He pointed to her stained slacks. "You'd better change those clothes."

Pulling at the fabric, Johanna stood and assessed the damage. "Yes, I suppose I should," she said, grateful for the excuse to hide away in her room. She turned at the doorway. "It's funny, really." She forced a nervous laugh. "Acting so childish over a little kiss. For heaven's sake, I've been married for ten years. We've known each other most of our lives. Tell me I'm being silly. Tell me it was just a kiss."

"If that's what you want to hear," he said.

She looked into his eyes. They were asking a question she wasn't quite prepared to answer. Not yet. "Yes," she said. "It is."

"Then, you're being silly, Johanna. It was just a kiss."

She took an audible deep breath, exhaled and smiled at him. He smiled back.

"Feel better?" he asked.

She nodded.

She looked so sweet, so vulnerable, he fought the urge to go to her, take her in his arms, kiss her again. Instead, he held his ground, stoically clenching his fists at his side.

"I think we'll both have to be a little patient with each other," he said.

Johanna grinned, thankful that he was making this easy for her. "You've never been a very patient person, Michael."

"No, that's true, but perhaps it's something I'm here to learn."

"Dealing with me may be your ultimate test," she teased.

"Maybe," he said as she left the room.

Truer words, he thought, had never been spoken.

Four

Michael didn't mean to be difficult, but after what happened last evening he felt the need to build some sort of barrier between Johanna and himself.

The furniture outlet was crowded to overflowing with the weekend shopping crowd, which made it easy to watch Johanna covertly. She was very conscientious in her role as decorator as she flipped through fabric books, matching, comparing and making decisions, which she optimistically presented to him and which he inevitably gave a thumbs-down.

Somehow furniture was just not a priority in his mind today.

She struggled to keep her frustration under wraps, as well as keep her distance, which suited him fine. Each time a salesperson mistook them for a couple, she would be the first to jump in with an indulgent laugh and an unmistakable correction. She was uptight and nervous, and wouldn't

look him in the eye. Which only reinforced his opinion of
the entire incident: Johanna had been caught off guard.
Johanna was frightened. Johanna had no desire to pursue
the subject of the kiss.

The kiss.

As if that was all that had been. As if he really could pretend that it hadn't happened the way it had. No matter how
she may have rationalized it away, try as he might, he
couldn't look at her the same way, not anymore, not since
his tongue had touched hers. Like a baby's first taste of ice
cream, bells had gone off in his brain, registering her special flavor, aroma and texture.

And he wanted more.

The craving he had for her had been born of a long-lost
youthful memory—a young girl had chased him until she'd
caught him. His ego had been bolstered by her attention
back then. But this was different. Last night shattered all
those illusions. Johanna, the woman, was infinitely more
desirable. The sad reality, though, was that Johanna, the
woman, was also no longer interested. She'd made that
perfectly clear. Just a silly kiss, she'd said. Comfort? Okay.
Companionship? Definitely. But more than that? Uh-uh.
No way.

So here he was, all grown-up, with a huge hankering for
a woman who didn't want him. How the tables had turned!
There was some sort of poetic justice hidden somewhere in
all this, he supposed, but for the life of him, he couldn't
enjoy the irony of it.

And therein was his dilemma. For even though his rational mind understood all of this, his body didn't give a
hoot. Just watching her move, lean forward, run her hands
over the fabric of the couch, sent tiny little messages that
bypassed his usually analytical brain and shot right to the
source of his desire.

And walking around all day with the source of his desire in this seemingly permanent condition was certainly a challenge he'd never had to face before.

She held up another piece of fabric, and this time he nodded and smiled, which reflected how bone tired he was rather than the fact that he liked the pattern. He'd had little to no sleep last night, and it was time to go home. Home. With Johanna, but not with Johanna.

It sure as hell was going to be another long night.

After eight hours of shopping, Johanna was about ready to give up. To put it mildly, she and Michael had distinctively different tastes in furniture. He hated the chintz couch she picked out, not to mention the tasseled lacquered fans for the living room. For some strange reason, he had it in his head to furnish the room in leather and chrome, which she abhorred.

Though she told herself it was his house and he should furnish it in whatever style he saw fit, she was determined to make her preferences known. She was able to convince him to compromise on the Oriental tea table, and he did concede that the multicolored throw pillows added a certain flair, but while she wanted a dozen, he thought two per couch was plenty.

The one thing they did agree on was the Southwestern motif for the den. It seemed to fit in so well with the light and color scheme of the room, and Michael fell in love with the geometric prints and earth tones.

All in all they accomplished a lot and, despite their differences, spent a very productive day. As if by silent agreement, they pretended that nothing had changed, as if the kiss they'd shared had been just as silly and innocent as she'd said and nothing more.

Johanna had even managed to convince herself that she had imagined most of it, or, at least, that her reaction had been more a one-sided *over*reaction. After all, other than his contrariness regarding the furniture, Michael seemed fine, totally oblivious to her discomfort and not at all chagrined. Unlike her. She made it a point to avoid his eyes when speaking to him, picking instead a sight just over his right shoulder.

By the end of the day, most of the furniture was on order. It was dark when they arrived home with take-out pizza. They sat at the kitchen counter and ate in silence, both too hungry to care that it was cold.

Michael dumped his paper dish in the trash and massaged the back of his neck. He was tired and stressed out from pretending. All he wanted to do was be alone right now, fall down somewhere and allow himself a reprieve, no matter how short, from his overactive body and mind.

"I'm beat," he said as he glanced at the empty den. "I wish that recliner was here right now."

Johanna finished eating the last bit of pizza. "It won't be long," she said. "It should be delivered within the next few weeks."

"I guess I've waited two years—another few weeks won't kill me," Michael said. "You look pretty tired yourself."

"*Exhausted* is a better word. I'm thinking about a nice hot tub right now."

"Have you tried the whirlpool in your bathroom yet?"

"No. It's been tempting me, though."

Michael pulled her off the stool and gently pushed her toward the door. "No time like the present to try. Go ahead, Johanna. Give yourself a treat and indulge yourself."

Johanna smiled over her shoulder and drew on her last vestiges of energy to climb the stairs. She ran her fingers through her hair and tied it up haphazardly into a ponytail on top of her head as she turned the taps and regulated the water. Finding some scented bubble bath under the sink, she sprinkled it in the water as she heard a knock on the door.

"Come in," she called.

Michael stood in the doorway. "You know how to work this thing?"

"Not really."

"Here, let me show you," he said as he insinuated himself between the tub and her. "How long do you want to soak?"

"I don't know—thirty minutes?"

Michael adjusted some knobs and set the timer. Immediately, the water began to churn and bubbles began to form. "All set."

He turned and almost bumped into her. They stood toe-to-toe, and he stared into her soulful hazel eyes. He scanned her face, choking back a myriad of unasked questions that seemed to hang between them as thick as the billows of steam rising from the tub.

He wanted to touch her. Simply, without much fanfare, he wanted to slowly strip the clothes off her body, piece by piece, and allow his hands to roam over her softness. Michael felt the tension claim him once again. His mouth tightened as if in pain. The reprieves, he was beginning to understand, would be agonizingly brief, and few and far between.

Yet still he couldn't stop himself from one tiny touch. He reached out with his index finger and followed the line of her face along her cheekbone to her chin. Her ponytail was in disarray, half up, half down. As he tucked a stray blond-streaked strand behind her ear, Johanna covered his hand with her own, guiding his motions. He didn't pull away, and neither did she.

The edges of the mirror began to fog, and Michael and Johanna became lost in a swirl of warm unreality. She felt the heat, inside and out. Every sensation became more pronounced—the intensity of his steel blue eyes and taut face, the sound of the rushing water, the feel of the steam permeating her skin, clouding her vision, swirling its way in and around her.

Exhaustion melted away, and building in its place was that dormant hunger which Michael's kiss had unleashed. It was real, and powerful, lurking too close to the surface for her to ignore. She wanted to touch and be touched. The thought of asking him to share the bath with her flitted through her mind, and with it came a pinch of desire in her belly so acute it bordered on pain. She could feel her blood rush through her veins as she blushed to her roots.

Michael watched her face metamorphose. He recognized that doe-caught-in-the-headlights look. She was uncomfortable with this kind of intimacy from him. He briefly wondered what had happened to that uninhibited teenage girl, then wondered further what kind of sex life she'd had with Jeff. He quickly tried to dismiss the thought. He could not—would not—allow himself to entertain that train of thought. Not if he wanted to maintain what was left of his sanity.

But the thought, once there, was impossible to dismiss. He pulled back—*When would he learn?*—and stepped around her.

"Enjoy, Johanna," he said softly. When she didn't move, he motioned toward the tub. "Go ahead. Before it gets cold."

Johanna lifted her hand toward him, but he missed the gesture and was gone before she could react. She turned to face her reflection in the remaining clear oval of the misty mirror. She almost didn't recognize the woman before her.

Desire was written in the lines of her face. She shut her eyes for a long moment, feeling dizzy, faint, confused and exhilarated all at the same time. Reaching for a towel, she patted her damp, curling hairline. When she opened them and caught her reflection once again, her face was pink with embarrassment.

Shaking herself out of her self-imposed stupor, she bent over to turn off the taps. Quickly, she shed her clothing and slowly sank down into the churning water.

Heavenly. Decadent. Sensual. The words skipped through her brain as the heat of the water penetrated every tense muscle. She leisurely glided her arms and legs back and forth to ensure each spot on her body was caressed by the jets of water. Rolling onto her stomach, she was buoyed by the bubbles as they danced over and under her.

But as the water began to revive the sensations of desire, she sat up, splashed the cooling water onto her face and hugged her knees to her chest. With the deepest of breaths, she fought her most basic needs. What was happening to her? Since her arrival at Michael's house, she'd become a different person. Celibacy had been a way a life for her for years now, and she had been fine, content, unbothered and unconcerned by her chaste state. Never once during her time with Jeff had she felt this powerful, urgent need to make love.

She picked up the washcloth and ran it over her overly sensitive skin, shutting her eyes, trying and failing to blot out the image of Michael's hands touching her....

The whirlpool jets stopped. It took Johanna a moment to realize that she was out of time. She dropped the cloth into the now cool water and watched the last of the bath bubbles crackle and die. Stepping out of the tub, she released the drain and wrapped herself in an oversize bath towel. She pulled the tie out of her ponytail and shook her hair free.

The bath had mellowed her, relaxed her to the point where she could hardly keep her eyes open. Towel wrapped securely around her, she walked into her bedroom and fell across the bed, thinking she'd rest for a minute or two before dressing and going back downstairs to face Michael.

No, she wasn't quite ready just yet to face Michael....

When she woke, it was almost midnight. Disoriented, Johanna sat up and rubbed her hands over her face, debating whether to get up or pull back the covers and climb in for the night. She shook off a chill, wishing for a cup of tea to warm her, and the decision seemed to be made. The towel was still wrapped around her. She pulled off the damp covering as she rose and slid open the closet door.

The royal blue negligee called out to her, but she ignored it. She was certain if she donned such a flimsy garment in her current state, she might lose whatever reserves of self-control she still managed to possess, march into his bedroom and throw herself down on his bed like a virgin on a sacrificial altar. Instead, she slipped into a gray-and-white warm-up suit which covered her from head to toe.

As she left her room, she noted that Michael's door was shut tightly. She hesitated on the steps. No light shone out from under the door, and she was sure he was asleep by now. He'd seemed so tired earlier, which may have been the reason for his reticence during the day. He certainly didn't need to deal with her strange mood tonight. She shook her head, admonishing herself, and made her way to the kitchen to make a cup of tea.

The kitchen was illuminated by a small night-light over the stove. Filling the teakettle, Johanna stood over it, waiting for the water to boil. She found some herb teas in a canister and picked out an orange spice flavor.

Clack!

The sound caused her to spill the hot water all over the counter. She checked over her shoulder for the source of the noise and noticed for the first time that the basement door was wide open, light spilling into the hall.

Johanna sopped up the water with a paper towel, then filled her cup and carried it with her as she satisfied her curiosity. Rounding the edge of the doorway, she peeked down the stairwell. Her feet bare, she padded down silently, stopping at the post at the base of the stairs.

Clack!

Johanna took the last step and turned. Michael was leaning over the oak-and-brass pool table, his head bowed in concentration as he angled for the best position. He seemed so intent, she didn't announce herself at first.

Michael made the shot, then lifted a brandy snifter off a serving table and toasted himself.

"Nice shot," she said.

The glass stopped midway to his lips. "Johanna."

She should be in bed. She should be sleeping. She should be anywhere but here. Her face was flushed fresh from sleep, the bath, or both; her hair was in disarray, and she looked lost in that baggy warm-up suit.

"Am I disturbing you?" she asked.

Hell, yes, he thought, but he said, "No, of course not. Come on down."

"I thought you were asleep in your room," she said.

Michael shrugged. "Couldn't sleep. Overtired, I guess. How about you? I thought you were out for the night."

"So did I, but I woke up." She lifted the cup of tea to her lips. "How about a game?" she asked.

Michael's eyebrows rose. "You play pool?"

"I used to."

"Sure," he said. "Why not?"

Johanna chose a medium-sized cue stick from the rack on the wall as Michael racked up the balls. She tested the feel of the stick. "I'll break," she said.

Michael grinned. "Be my guest."

The cue stick felt awkward in her hands as she chalked the tip. It had been quite a few years since she'd played. Early in Jeff's career, he supported them by hustling in pool halls. She'd picked up a thing or two and had become fairly proficient at the game.

She wasn't about to tell Michael that. Strangely, she was loath to talk about Jeff with him. It wasn't that it made her sad—quite the contrary. Jeff had been her best friend, and she had many fond memories of her time with him, especially early on in the marriage.

But she didn't feel comfortable talking about Jeff to Michael, and, as if there were some unspoken rule, he rarely mentioned Jeff's name to her. That is, other than to ask her questions about the accident...questions she had managed to avoid answering.

She bent over the table as she lined up the cue ball. Then she very carefully aimed, struck out...and missed. Not once, but twice.

"Are you sure you know how to play this game?" Michael asked.

Johanna stood erect. "Yes, I'm sure."

She rested her chin on the fist that held the cue stick. She stared at the table, contemplating what she did wrong when Michael came up behind her.

"Need some help?"

He was so close, his breath skimmed her neck. She shivered inwardly, fighting a desire to lean back into him. "No. I can do this. I can beat you, too."

"Willing to bet?"

She looked at him over her shoulder. "Money?"

He shrugged. "What else have you got to offer?"

Johanna's face flamed instantly, and Michael bit his tongue. When would he stop doing this? When would he stop putting her in these awkward positions?

"How about a dinner?" he added hastily.

Johanna made a face. "I always cook dinner."

"Okay, then lunch. Loser buys lunch."

"I think I can handle that."

Johanna retried the shot and this time broke perfectly, sinking a ball.

"Pretty good," he said.

"Thanks."

Michael leaned against the opposite end of the table to get a bird's-eye view of her effort. Johanna smiled at him, then unconsciously tugged on her sweatshirt, which let him know in no uncertain terms that her breasts were free and unrestricted underneath. He shifted uncomfortably. Then she picked up the blue chalk and began to slowly, intently—and, to Michael, almost lovingly—rub the tip of the cue stick with it. At the same time, the tip of her tongue poked out of her mouth as she licked her bottom lip in concentration.

Michael was mesmerized. His imagination was having a wild time. He could almost feel each stroke of her fingertips and tongue on selected parts of his own body, and he was becoming irrationally jealous of the attention she was giving that inanimate cue stick.

Johanna glanced his way as she prepared to take aim. He was staring at her. "Am I doing something wrong?" she asked.

"What?"

"You were staring at me. Is something wrong with this shot?"

Michael didn't dare move. His body was hot, tight and hard. It took all his effort to keep his face blank, his eyes neutral.

"Uh, no. You're fine. Fine."

Johanna tilted her head and gave him a puzzled look before returning her attention to her shot. As she leaned over the table, her scent drifted to him, a soft, rosewater fragrance from her bath. The image she must have made relaxing in the whirlpool flashed through his mind.

He stood and walked over to the other corner of the table. This wasn't working...nothing was working. He wanted her, desired her, lusted for her...felt things he shouldn't feel for her.

After sinking two solid balls, Johanna missed. "Your turn," she said, stepping back to give him room.

Michael pushed himself to act. He studied the table, pointed his stick toward the far end and said, "Ten ball, corner."

Johanna watched him sink the striped ball. She found herself caressing him with her eyes, scanning his broad shoulders, his back, the line of his solid buttocks and thighs. He was long, lean and so beautifully built, her insides were warmed just by looking at him.

Was it her imagination, or was he getting better by the day? Maybe it was all that heavy-duty working out he did each night. She didn't know he'd been that prone to exercise, but then, she didn't really know very much about him at all. In some ways, she felt she knew him so well, and in others, he remained a deep mystery.

Like tonight. He was the normally reserved, controlled Michael she'd come to know, yet she'd caught him staring at her several times in a way that could only be described as blatantly sexual. She wasn't so far gone that she didn't recognize that look in a man's eyes. He could control his words, but not those steely blues—they were blazing with the same hunger that had invaded her system in the tub upstairs.

Could he be hungering for her? Her heart began to beat rapidly with the thought. What if that were true? What if he did indeed want her the way she wanted him? The thought of making love with him made her knees weak, and she gripped the edge of the pool table for support.

She would love to find out, love to give him a sign, tempt him to act on his desire. It would be so wonderful, she knew that it would—better, more fulfilling, than that first time.

But what if she did just that? What if they made love and then she discovered that it was *all* he wanted from her?

Oh, Lord, she couldn't bear that... not again. She couldn't let herself go, give in to her needs, couldn't allow herself to discover the truth, because the truth could hurt her so much more than the hunger.

Michael sank three more before missing. "You're up."

Johanna bit her lip. She didn't feel like playing pool anymore. She didn't feel like doing anything except hiding away from him, from herself. Without paying much attention, she aimed and missed.

"You're not concentrating, Johanna," Michael said.

He took his turn, sank the remainder of the striped balls, then the eight ball. "Game," he said, then cleared the table of hers as well.

Johanna placed her cue stick back into the wall rack. "You win," she said. "I owe you one lunch. Should I write it out and sign it?"

Michael moved behind her, leaned over her as he replaced his cue stick next to hers. "I trust you," he said.

She turned to face him. "Do you?"

"Shouldn't I?"

"I don't know." Johanna lowered her head so she wouldn't have to feel the scrutiny of his eyes. "Sometimes I don't trust myself."

They were standing close together, so very close he could count her eyelashes. He reached up and held her shoulders. "What is it, Johanna?"

"It's me. And you. What happened last night—"

"I said I was sorry. We were talking about Jeff, and things got a little emotional for you. It's going to happen, Johanna. It just got a little carried away."

"I know. That's just it...."

"Yes?"

Johanna looked up at him, her eyes wide, glowing with an intensity she couldn't know, could only feel. "I liked it."

Michael felt his heart slam against his chest wall. "What are you saying, Johanna?"

"I'm saying I liked it when you kissed me. I liked the way it made me feel, and..."

"And what?"

"And I want to kiss you again."

Michael dropped his hands. "I don't think that's such a good idea," he said, taking a much-needed step back.

Johanna followed with a step forward. "Why not?"

"Because what happened last night will happen again. I can't promise you it'll end with a kiss."

Johanna wet her lips with the tip of her tongue. "So? I can handle it."

He made a sound that could have been a laugh, but didn't quite make it. "Can you?" He reached up and threaded his fingers through her hair. "I can't."

"Oh, Michael..." She parted her lips.

"Johanna, I'm not made of stone."

She reached up and touched his chest ever so lightly with her fingertips. "I know...."

It was all too much for him. With a groan, he accepted the invitation of her lips, her eyes, her woman's scent, and kissed her. At first he only brushed his lips against hers, but then their mouths melded together so naturally, it seemed as if they were two parts to a puzzle.

He pulled her to him, and she wrapped her arms around his waist. It was as if the kiss last night were a rehearsal, and this was the real thing. He deepened the kiss, exploring the soft insides of her mouth with his tongue...and then the tip of her tongue touched his and all rational thought left him.

He moved his hands over her back, under her top, feeling her soft skin, driving himself wild with need.

Johanna melted under his touch. She had never felt like this before—so sensitive, so alive, yet so weak with pleasure. Her knees gave out, and she reached up around him to cling to his shoulders for support. He spun her around and lifted her up onto the pool table, positioning himself between her legs. Instinctively, she wrapped her ankles around his thighs, and pressed herself into his hardness.

Michael ran his hands up her sides and brushed the fullness of her breasts with his knuckles. And then he did what he had been longing to do. He cupped her with his palms and gently massaged each soft mound in tandem. He broke the kiss, needing to savor this moment, needing all his energy, all his concentration to absorb the pleasure of how she felt in his hands.

Johanna buried her face in his neck as he rubbed his thumbs rhythmically back and forth across her sensitized nipples. She felt like a rag doll—limp and longing to be played with. And he obliged her until she was unaware of who she was or where she was, only how she felt...and what she needed.

"Michael," she moaned, "I need..." She looked up at him. "Please..."

Michael angled his head and took her mouth with wet, hot hunger. Their tongues met, mated in a frenzy of desire neither could control. He reached down with one hand, insinuating his fingers into the elastic waistband of her pants, rubbing the backs of his knuckles against her abdomen until he came in contact with the source of her desire. He threaded his fingers through her soft nest of curls, reveling in the moist heat he found there...for him, all for him.

Johanna's heart was beating so hard she could hear her blood pulse through her veins. Wantonly, she spread her legs farther to give him better access. Not caring how she looked or what she was doing, she lifted her hips almost off the table in an attempt to guide his fingers to the one spot where she needed him the most.

And then he found her. She began to whimper as he stroked her, back and forth, back and forth, until she could no longer breathe. She broke from kissing him, resting her forehead against his chest as he continued his heavenly assault on her senses.

The tiny sounds she was making were driving him crazy, but he continued to touch her, growing bolder with his fingers as she arched into him. She was swollen, hot and oh, so wet against his hand, and he knew she was almost there....

"Come on, Johanna," he whispered. "Don't stop...."

And then it happened. The room, the very world around her, exploded inside her brain. She threw her head back and called out his name, over and over again, begging him to stop this insane pleasure that was so intense it bordered on pain.

But he didn't stop, not until it was over, not until the last tremor racked her body, not until she was totally and completely satisfied.

She couldn't look at him. What could he be thinking of her? She'd joked about being a sex-starved widow who hadn't had a man in too long a time, but was that really so far from the truth?

She was beyond embarrassed.

Because she'd made a fool of herself.

With Michael.

Again.

He lifted her chin. "Johanna?"

"Yes."

"Are you all right?"

She shut her eyes and shook her head. "How can you ask that?"

"I wanted to be sure."

Johanna looked at him. "Are *you* all right? I can... I mean, if you want—"

"I'm fine," he said.

Which wasn't in the least bit true. He was burning from the inside out, but he wasn't about to let her satisfy him out of some misplaced sense of fair play. No, when—and if—that ever took place, it would have to be because she wanted more than just a temporary release.

He did his poor body a favor and took a step back from her, held out his hand and helped her off the pool table.

Johanna ran her fingers through her tousled hair and adjusted her warm-up suit. She managed a faint smile. "I don't know what you can be thinking of me—"

"Go on up, Johanna," he said before she could apologize, which he was sure she was going to attempt to do.

"But—"

"Please."

As if she instinctively knew that it would be wiser to obey him this time, Johanna mumbled a hasty good-night and scurried up the stairs.

Michael waited until he heard her footsteps fade, then lifted a cue stick off the rack. He checked the table. All that he'd left was the cue ball. He measured, leaned over it, then stood behind it as he aimed. With one resounding smack, it flew across the felt table, but bumped into the sides and swiftly came right back at him.

He allowed himself a wry grin as he picked up the cue ball. He tossed it in the air and then replaced it on the table. He couldn't go to bed. Not now. Not with Johanna still awake and only a few unprotected steps away from his room. He wasn't that strong.

Instead, Michael ambled over to the other side of the basement. He was wound tight, filled with a sexual energy that demanded some kind of release. He thought about going out, but there was nowhere he wanted to go and no one he wanted to be with.

Well, the only person he wanted to be with had already made the offer. He'd chosen against that, declining not out of any warped sense of self-sacrifice, but because he already knew what she'd claimed was true—it had been a long time for her.

No, next time, if there was a next time, she had to want *him,* not some substitute to satisfy a long-suppressed need.

In the meantime, he'd do what he'd said he would do. He'd be patient . . . and maybe work out for a while.

Five

Johanna didn't go to Michael's office to help out at all the following week. She'd already broken every vow she'd made to herself where he was concerned. She could barely face him since her unbelievably bawdy behavior Saturday night. Living in the same house made it more than difficult to avoid him, but she managed to keep their exchanges to a minimum. Luckily, Michael was preoccupied with his presentation and didn't seem to notice.

She spent the better part of her time cleaning house, readying everything for the furniture delivery. Yet even the physical activity couldn't stop her mind from working overtime. No matter how much she lectured herself about what she'd done, she couldn't deny the results. Every basic instinct she owned was screaming out to her at every turn. She tried not to listen, but her mind couldn't let go of it. The voice in her ear was persistent, incessant and impossible to ignore.

Michael wanted her.

After Saturday night, she could no longer pretend that she'd gone to him for comfort and nothing else. That first kiss may have been just that, but the second time... The way he kissed her, touched her, the way she'd opened herself to him, could not be reasoned away so easily.

Johanna was not a child. She could dismiss a look, a touch, even a kiss, but when a man was aroused, there were certain things that couldn't be explained away, and Michael had met *all* the criteria. But while that should have inspired hope in her eager heart, all it did was terrify her. Her fear was age-old and particularly potent because she'd played this scene with him before, and to devastating effect.

The days were long gone when she tried to kid herself that Michael's rejection had nothing to do with her elopement with Jeff. In her heart of hearts, she knew it had. The things he'd said to her that morning in her mother's kitchen had shattered her dreams, adolescent though they may have been.

Since the moment she'd laid eyes on Michael Ross at twelve years old, Johanna had set her mind to having him in her life.

And not as her brother-in-law.

Making love with him the night of the block party had been the culmination of everything she'd yearned for. She'd truly believed that she and Michael would be together from that day forward. When it all fell apart the next morning, it had wiped out every coherent thought, every plan, every goal she had set for herself. There was no past, no present, no future, only a blank void looming ahead of her.

She had allowed Jeff to fill that void, not out of love, but out of indifference: she just plain hadn't cared anymore.

It had taken years for that numbness to wear off. Once it had, she rebuilt her life as best she could, worked on her marriage as best she could, and even admitted her mistake when it was no longer possible to pretend.

She'd come so far, beyond the hurt, beyond the indifference, even beyond the horror of Jeff's death. She couldn't—wouldn't—put herself back in that vulnerable position. She *couldn't* fall in love with Michael Ross again, not if there was one chance in a million that he didn't feel the same way.

And that was the problem. She had no idea what he was feeling or thinking. He'd always had that ability to hide behind his deep blue eyes. And since that episode on the pool table, his guard was up, and he was constantly on the alert with her. He picked his words carefully and was exceedingly polite. So polite that Johanna was convinced if he said "please" and she said "thank you" one one more time, she would surely be sick to her stomach.

And, worst of all, he was distant...always, always distant.

Except when they touched. He lost that iron-clad self-control. His body's communication techniques were state-of-the-art and crystal clear.

So what was the truth? Was he her dutiful brother-in-law with a clear-cut plan to help her get back on her feet again emotionally and financially? Or was he attracted to her as a woman, desiring her as a woman, wanting a relationship with her as a woman? Or did it just end with the desire?

And how could she discover the truth without being hurt in the process?

Though she was confused and more than a little frightened by what was happening, she was also strangely excited, too. She felt as if she were embarking on a new adventure. And she was not unhappy. Quite the contrary, she had been walking on cloud nine ever since *it* had happened.

Funny, but she'd never been particularly consumed by *it* as some women were. She'd never picked up a magazine to read an article expounding on her right to have *it*, nor was she overly concerned that her experience in that area of life—while adequate—had been limited, to say the least.

But after her powerful response to his touch, she understood what the fuss was all about, and for the life of her she couldn't keep herself from grinning. At odd times. Like in the shower. Or in line at the supermarket or bank. She was sure people thought her mad or, hopefully, just a little eccentric. Thank goodness they couldn't know exactly what thoughts were putting that smile on her face.

The only place she was determined to maintain her cool was when she was around Michael. And since she had little control over herself these days, the best course of action seemed to be to stay clear of him.

But by the following Tuesday she was antsy. Her first night class was scheduled that evening, and she was so excited about the prospect, she had to share it with someone, even Michael . . . especially Michael.

Johanna decided to surprise him at work. Her rationalizations were valid, she decided. She wouldn't be around for dinner, and, besides, she owed him a lunch. It would also be a great opportunity, in the neutral surroundings of his office, to smooth over the awkwardness they were feeling around each other.

She packed all the fixings for a picnic into a basket, including her homemade fried chicken left over from the night before and a chocolate cake she'd baked. She even stopped at the deli to pick up some salads.

When she arrived at the office, Michael's receptionist was out to lunch, so she let herself into his inner office with a short knock.

He was not alone, and by the look on his face, he was none too happy with her interruption, either.

"Oh, I'm sorry," she said as she brought her hand to her mouth. "Excuse me. I'll come back later."

"No, please come in now," the older man said, standing as she entered the room. He held out his hand. "I'm Jack Larsen. And you're . . . ?"

"Johanna Ross," she said as she shook his hand.

His name was familiar. This was the Texan Michael had told her about, his new client—or, at least, the new client he'd hoped to sign. Oh, Lord! She'd interrupted the all-important presentation he'd been working on for the past few months.

Having not spoken more than two sentences at a time to him this week, she'd had no idea that today was the big day. She felt awful about barging in like this, knowing how important this was to him. It just went to prove how out-of-it she was where he was concerned. How could she not have called first?

She mouthed "I'm sorry" over Mr. Larsen's head, and Michael returned a quick, tight smile of forgiveness.

"Johanna, what can I do for you?" he asked pleasantly enough, but she knew by the tautness of his jawline that he wanted her to leave. Now.

"Nothing important," she said. "I was just in the neighborhood—"

"Whatcha got there?" Mr. Larsen asked, pointing to the picnic basket. "Looks like lunch to me."

"Well, it is. A picnic lunch. Sort of." She smiled at the dour-faced Michael.

"That was a great idea, Johanna, but we're right in the middle of a meeting. Maybe some other time."

"Of course—"

"Enough in there for three?" Mr. Larsen asked.

"Er . . . yes, there is."

"Great. Let's take a break, Ross, and get a taste of your pretty little wife's fixings."

"She's not my—"

"I'm not his—"

"—wife."

"—wife."

Johanna's and Michael's eyes met, and what was becoming an all-too-familiar spark flashed between them. She tried to look away, to return her attention to the older gentleman, but for the life of her, she could not. Michael's eyes held her like a laser beam.

If she hadn't known better, she'd have said his look was thick with the same kind of longing that filled her heart. She had the strongest desire to reach across the desk to him, kiss his mouth the way he had kissed hers and start the whole seductive process again. Her body throbbed with the memory of his gentle touch. And more than anything, she wanted to sample that bittersweet ache again.

He must have read her thoughts, because his look changed to one of warning. *Not now, Johanna,* it said. But she, in turn, sent a message of her own which clearly stated her feelings on the matter. "When, Michael?"

Jack Larsen cleared his throat, and Johanna forced her attention to him. Without losing a beat, she reintroduced herself.

"I was married to Michael's brother, Jeff," she said. "I'm his widow."

"I'm sorry for the mistake and for your loss," Jack Larsen said as he eyed them both for a long moment.

Johanna smiled. "It's quite all right. Everyone does it."

"Well," he continued, slapping his hand on his thigh, "whatcha got in that basket, Johanna? I *can* call you Johanna, can't I?"

She smiled at him. "Of course, and I'll call you Jack, okay?"

"Sure thing. Now let's eat. I'm starving. This boy's kept me working all morning."

"I'm sorry, Mr. Larsen," Michael said as he checked his watch. "I guess it is lunchtime. Where would you like to go?"

"What's wrong with right here?" Jack said.

Johanna smiled. She liked this man. He was friendly, open, and though she knew the folksy manner probably hid a very tough, shrewd businessman, her instincts told her he was fair and trustworthy, as well. He would be good for Michael, and, prejudiced though she was, she was equally sure that Michael would be good for him.

He seemed to like her, and if she could help that process a little, she saw no reason not to. If there was one thing she'd learned traveling around the country with Jeff, it was how to get along with strangers. She'd acquired the ability to have a friendly conversation with just about anyone and be perfectly comfortable doing so.

She knew she complemented Michael in that way. While he was a genius for facts and figures, she had good social instincts. With a little luck, she might be able to redeem herself and turn this disastrous interruption into something positive for him.

She smiled at Michael and proceeded to unpack the picnic basket.

Michael came around his desk and stopped in front of Johanna as she laid out the contents of the basket. As annoyed as he was at her right now, he couldn't help but feel glad to see her. She looked fabulous to his Johanna-starved eyes. She'd stopped coming down to breakfast this week, and he couldn't believe how much he missed her being there.

She'd been avoiding him, and, of course, he knew why.

Saturday night had wiped him out, too. No amount of exercise had been able to tamp down this hunger. He could not ever remember having such an erotic experience with a woman, one that had so emotionally satisfied him while leaving him so tightly wound physically.

He knew Johanna was embarrassed by what happened. He should be, too, if he had any sense. But he wasn't. Not in the least. Instead, he was ridiculously proud of the way he'd made her respond to him, to her own body's needs. But as good as the experience made him feel, it also dredged up a lot of old feelings he'd have preferred never to have to deal with again. Unfortunately, like everything else in his life lately, he couldn't control them.

He'd spent the better part of the week analyzing the incident from every aspect and every angle. He explained it away in a hundred ways: she was lonely, she was tired, she was caught off guard, she needed someone, and he just happened to be the one available. None satisfied him, and none really dealt with the core issue, for deep down, no matter how hard he tried, he couldn't stop himself from wondering about her and Jeff.

It was useless. It was painful. It was frustrating. It evoked all his old jealousies, but he couldn't help himself. She had responded to him so naturally, with such uninhibited passion, she couldn't be faking it. What had happened to Johanna had been real.

But was it different? Special?

The questions had lingered long after she'd gone to bed that night, and days after when she avoided his eyes. He wanted it to be different, very different, and he wanted it to be more special than anything she had ever experienced in her life. Silly, yes. Macho, probably. But in his mind it should have been so wonderfully special that she would never forget him . . . or confuse him.

And whether he liked to admit it or not, that was the crux of the problem. Though he might have been her first lover, she had spent the better part of the last ten years as his brother's wife. While he could pretend that it didn't bother him, his inner soul knew better. It bothered him. Big-time.

He was a pretty straightforward kind of guy. He wanted more than a kiss here, a caress there. He wanted her in every elemental way he could think of. And then some. Problem was, three in a bed—even if the third party was Jeff's ghost—just didn't do it for him.

His rational mind told him to let it go, let sleeping dogs lie. Back off and let her be. Retreat to Plan One and help Johanna get herself back on her feet so she could get on with her life.

So she could move out.

It was the smart thing to do, the wise choice in a no-win situation, and he made a conscious pact with himself in the middle of one of those never-ending, sleepless nights to do just that. To keep Johanna at arm's length from now on.

But, as usual, Johanna wasn't cooperating with his plan. Now, into his office she'd waltzed with the sweetest smile on her face and a basketful of fried chicken on her arm. How could he fight her? How could he fight himself when every fiber of his being responded to her like a flowering plant responding to the light of a springtime sun?

When he'd seen her at his office door, he'd wanted to hug her and strangle her at the same time. He attempted a smile at Jack Larsen as the man helped Johanna spread a blue-and-white-checkered tablecloth onto the floor. The big Texan seemed charmed by her. The two of them chatted away about the weather and the rush-rush attitude of the people in the East, as if they'd known each other for years.

How did she do that? How did she take an ordinary situation and make it seem like a holiday? How did she suddenly turn his office into a cozy parlor? And how did she warm his heart by just looking at her?

"Can't you get this boy to relax a little?" Jack asked. He was seated cross-legged on the floor munching on a chicken leg, which he poked in Michael's direction as he made his point. "Can't trust a man who doesn't know how to have fun."

Johanna noted Michael's pensive mood. She chuckled at Jack. "Oh, he knows how to have fun all right."

Boldly, she reached over to Michael and did something she'd itched to do since her arrival. She stuck her finger in his collar and loosened his tie. He pulled back, but she didn't let that deter her. She leaned forward and unbuttoned the top button of his shirt. Then, slowly, softly, she ran her hand gently inside his collar. She felt his response in the tips of her fingers; she read his response in his eyes. Both cheered her enormously.

"There, you see," she said to Jack. "All relaxed. Believe me, Jack, you can trust Michael with your business." Michael reached up and took hold of her hand before she could pull it away. Their fingers intertwined. Their gazes locked. And her heart flipped over in her chest. "I trust him with my life."

"Hoo-wee!" Jack said, slapping his thigh as Michael released Johanna's hand. "This little lady sure is the best salesperson you've got here, Ross. Hope you appreciate her."

"Oh, I appreciate her all right," Michael said, his voice tinged with resignation. What's the use? he asked himself. You can't fight her because you can't fight yourself. And because deep down . . . you don't really want to.

They finished eating. Johanna nibbled. Michael picked. And Jack wolfed down everything else in sight. He patted his belly when he was done.

"Did you make all this yourself?" he asked Johanna.

"Most of it."

"Mighty tasty. I sure miss Donna Sue's cookin' when we're away from home. All that fancy restaurant food—" he waved his hand in dismissal "—for my money, you can keep it."

"Isn't your wife traveling with you?"

"Matter of fact, she's doing just that. She's getting in some Fifth Avenue shopping while I finish my business."

"If you're looking for a home-cooked meal, we'd love to have both of you for dinner before you leave, Mr. Larsen," Michael asked.

"Now if Johanna here is calling me Jack, you have to call me Jack, too."

"Jack, then. Seriously, Johanna and I would be honored if you would come to dinner. I can attest to the fact that she makes a great roast."

"Please do, Jack."

Jack Larsen looked from Johanna to Michael and back again. "Well, I can't see how I can refuse such an offer. When is a good time for y'all?"

"Anytime," Johanna said. "Let your wife pick a date."

"Sounds great. I'll do just that," Jack said.

Johanna smiled at Michael, and he nodded his approval. She felt as if she'd accomplished something, something vastly more important than just arranging a dinner party. The pensive look in Michael's eyes was gone, replaced by one that warmed her heart. For the life of her, she had to admit that she wanted to do things for him that would make him look at her that way more often.

A good way to start, she thought, would be by not overstaying her welcome.

"Well, gentlemen, this was a pleasure, but I think it's time you got back to work, and I get myself ready for school this evening," she said.

She scooped up all the picnic paraphernalia, and the two men helped as she repacked.

"I look forward to our dinner," Jack said. "I think you and Donna Sue are gonna get along just fine."

"I'm sure we will," Johanna said, shaking his hand goodbye.

Michael escorted her out of his office and into the reception area. He pulled her to a stop by the outer doorway.

"Tonight's your first class, isn't it?" he asked.

"Yes, I'm really excited," Johanna said as she placed the picnic basket at her feet. Then she reached up to readjust his tie. "But I won't be home for dinner."

He stood still for her ministrations. "Don't worry about me," he said with a self-deprecating grin, "I'll be fine on my own. After the stress of this meeting, I'll probably crash early, anyway."

Johanna reached down and lifted the picnic basket. "I can leave something in the fridge."

"Don't bother. Just take care of yourself." He held open the outer door for her. "Good luck tonight," he said.

"You, too," she whispered conspiratorially, nodding in the direction of his office.

"Thanks," he said, then grabbed hold of her arm to stop her from leaving. "For everything. You were great in there."

"Oh? And I was going to apologize for barging in unannounced. You didn't look too happy to see me initially."

"Initially, I wasn't. But you have a unique ability, Johanna," he said, a half grin on his face.

"And what ability is that?" she asked, her pleasure at his pleasure shining through.

His smile faded. "To make every place your own. Like you belong there. Like everywhere you are is . . . home."

Johanna didn't know how to answer him, so she remained silent. Michael reached up and caressed the side of her face with his hand. Like a puppy, she leaned into his palm.

They stood that way for what seemed like the longest time, but was no more than a matter of seconds.

And then, to her surprise, he leaned down and kissed her, a gentle brushing of his lips against hers, as if it were the most natural thing in the world to do.

"Go, Johanna," he said softly before turning his back to her and entering his office.

The door shut behind him, leaving Johanna alone. Leaning against the open door, she reached up and patted her lips with the tips of her fingers, outlining their shape, caressing the spot where his lips had been.

Lord, she was in really bad shape! All it took was a look, a touch from him, to cause her head to spin like a merry-go-round gone crazy. She wanted to call him back, wanted to pour out her heart to him, tell him so many things she had kept tucked away for so long. But that was impossible, not just because of where they were, but because of who she was and who he was and what had happened in their lives to bring them to this point.

She walked out of the office and got into the car, but her mind was racing.

There was so much between them. Some might say too much to overcome. But, besides the guilt she harbored and the obligations he felt, or any of the other myriad things that forced them to keep their distance, there was really only one barrier that stood between them like a fortress.

His brother.

Her husband.

Jeff.

He wouldn't have wanted to be that barrier—she knew that in her heart of hearts. He was her best friend for too

many years for her not to know how and what he thought
about himself. Sometimes she felt she knew Jeff better than
herself. She'd loved him like a brother, which was almost
laughably sad because it was Michael for whom she should
have had those feelings. But such was not the case, not ever,
though she'd tried her best to insure that Jeff never knew it.

But he no doubt knew it now, and she would bet her life
on the fact that he would have hated playing the martyr.
Then why did she cast him that way? Why did Michael?
Why were they dancing around the issue of Jeff?

She had to admit she was the one doing the dancing. If
anything, Michael had tried to initiate conversations about
Jeff, but she had changed the subject or replied with flip,
one-word, end-of-conversation answers.

But she couldn't help that. She might be over Jeff's death,
but not her part in it. It was still there, deep down, buried,
but alive enough to erupt every now and then, like a dormant but dangerous volcano. She didn't want to tell Michael about their argument. She had no idea what Michael
thought about her marriage, but she still couldn't bring
herself to reveal the truth about it. Not to anyone, but *absolutely* not to Michael.

It made her feel like such a fool, such a failure, such a
fraud. Here she was getting herself back together again,
going back to school to try to make something of her life.
How could she admit that her marriage was a sham? How
could she admit that she had been too cowardly to do anything about it? And how could she admit that when she finally took the initiative and tried to end it, the effect had
been his only brother's death?

The guilt was still there, strong and controlling as ever.

Jeff would tell her to give it up. Don't sweat it. He was,
if anything at all, a free spirit, believing everyone should
follow their heart. If he were here right now, standing beside her, he'd tell her to "go for it, babe."

But she had never been as free as Jeff.

And what about Michael? Could he let go, forget the past, forget the roadblocks they had in their way? Could he get beyond Jeff and see her not as his brother's wife, but just as Johanna, a woman who wanted him more than anything she had ever wanted in her life?

She shut her eyes, fighting back feelings that were surfacing at a fast and furious rate. He meant so much to her, in so many ways, and she knew that whatever the outcome of all this, he would forever hold a special place in her heart. Yet the thought of leaving him, of moving away again, brought desolation in its wake.

While at first she scoffed at the idea of Michael needing her—needing anyone—she knew now that whether he would admit it or not, he would feel the same way.

A wave of emotion swept over her, and with it came a realization of something that had never entered her mind.

Michael was as lonely as she.

Seeing him in this setting, where he was all business, only seemed to highlight the fact, so much more so than when he was at home in his big, empty house.

Yes, Michael was lonely. He didn't know it, of course, and would argue with her if she ever had the nerve to tell him so.

Johanna started the engine and put the car in gear. She had to take this thought home, chew on it before she would be able to decide what her next course of action should be.

It was a question that had been on her mind since last Saturday night, and it demanded an answer, a plan, a resolution.

So, Johanna, she asked herself as she pulled into the traffic, where do you go from here?

Six

By her second week at college Johanna felt as if she'd never left school. She loved her classes, and she loved the teachers, especially her English teacher, a burly bear of a man with a full white beard who was earthy to the core. He made her blush with his constant poetic quotations regarding the slings and arrows of unrequited love, a subject she felt well versed in since her arrival at Michael's home. But he made learning fun, and Johanna couldn't remember that ever being the case for her. Another example, she supposed, of the difference between wanting to do something and having to do it.

She had also met two women who, like her, were returning for their degrees. They planned to sit together each week and exchanged telephone numbers. Though she felt awkward talking about herself at first, Johanna managed to get through the question "So you live with your brother-in-law?'' without too much trouble, and she was looking forward to forming new friendships.

The following week Michael was away on business. He had to go to Boston for a series of meetings. Johanna was loath to go home to the quiet, empty house, so she was grateful for her new friends' offer to go out for coffee.

It was almost eleven by the time she arrived home. She had hoped he might be back, but when she let herself in, the house was still. The night-light she'd left on over the stove lured her toward the kitchen. She snapped on the answering machine and scribbled two messages for Michael before walking into the den and turning on the dimmer for the high-hat lights over the fireplace.

The last message was from Michael.

"Hi," his voice said.

"Hi," she said back to the machine.

"Meetings were endless. It doesn't look like I'll be able to get back tonight. I'll call you in the morning. Hope your class went well." There was a staticky pause, then, "Good night, Johanna."

"Good night, Michael." She hit the rewind button. "Oh, well," she said out loud.

Her voice echoed off the walls of the almost empty room. Almost empty except for the beat-up old couch. She never did get around to asking Michael why it was the only piece of furniture he had. Not that it mattered. The new furniture was due to be delivered, and the old couch would be carted away, never to be seen again. Shrugging, she sauntered into the kitchen and pulled open the refrigerator door. Mindlessly, she stared at the contents.

She wasn't the least bit tired. She was riding a natural high and had no desire to call it a night yet. In fact, she felt more like partying than sleeping. It was strange how her memories of high school registered as a blur of boredom, but her classes now only seemed to exhilarate her.

A bottle of wine was lying on its side. She lifted it and examined the label. It was Michael's favorite Chardonnay, and she nodded her approval. She uncorked the bottle and poured herself a glass. After two sips, she carried the goblet with her as she climbed the stairs.

Out of habit, she checked Michael's room. The door was slightly open and the room depressingly dark. It was strange how she missed him. He'd only been gone two days, and already she was having withdrawal pains. At times like this it was hard to remember that he didn't belong to her, that she was only a visitor on borrowed time. She shook her head at her own foolishness as she made her way to her own room.

Enjoying her absolute privacy, Johanna stripped off her clothes with the door open wide, throwing each garment haphazardly around the room. Tomorrow, she promised herself, she would clean up meticulously, but tonight she wanted to let herself go.

She took a quick shower and washed her hair, wrapping it in a towel on top of her head. Turning on the television, she watched the news as she pampered herself by applying a scented lotion to every inch of her body within reach, after which she took time she never seemed to have to polish her toenails.

She padded naked to her closet. Resting her weight on her hip, she held the wine goblet in one hand and flipped through her clothes with the other. She wanted something light, as carefree, silky smooth and feminine as she felt right now.

She frowned when nothing struck her fancy. A Chinese silk kimono embroidered with a grand benevolent dragon would fit her mood, she decided, but she didn't own one.

The closest thing she had to such a thing was the new royal blue robe that matched the negligee Michael had bought her.

As she sipped the wine, Johanna pulled it out and held it up for inspection. It was soft, feminine, but still practical and not nearly as sexually blatant as the negligee. Which was fine. Placing the goblet on the end table, she donned the robe, then admired her reflection in the full-length closet-door mirror. She twisted and turned. It seemed a little too elegant to wear for no special occasion, but since she was alone, she saw no harm in indulging herself.

The material slid against her supple skin, and that cinched it. Taking another sip of wine, Johanna unwrapped her hair from the towel and shook it out, deciding to let it dry naturally. She began humming to herself, missing for the first time in a long time the music that had so surrounded her life for the last ten years.

Which sparked an idea. Pulling her duffel bag out of the closet, she rummaged through it until she found her jazz tapes. The instrumental music was sweetly different from the hard rock that Jeff had played. Listening to it had seemed almost therapeutic after his death, and now she was a real fan.

She finished the last drop of wine and carried the empty glass and two tapes back downstairs. Turning on the stereo, she slipped in the first tape, setting the volume loud enough that it bounced off the walls and filled the house. The music drifted around her, and, pleased with her ingenuity, Johanna glided into the kitchen on the strains of Kenny G's soprano saxophone.

As she hummed along with the familiar music, she poured another glass of wine. If nothing else, she would sleep well tonight. She found several votive candles in the cabinet under the sink, lit them and turned out all the lights. Glass aloft, she glided into the center of the den and swayed to the haunting sounds that always seemed to reach deep down and grab her soul with both hands.

Except for the glamorous robe and the absence of a cigarette in her hand, the entire scene brought back memories of the early days after Jeff's death. Alone and lonely, Johanna would lose herself in the music. It had seemed so necessary at the time to hide inside herself, and the music had helped. While she didn't feel so bleakly alone anymore, she had to admit she still nurtured a certain *aloneness.*

In that way she and Michael had a lot in common. She had been giving a lot of thought to her analysis of Michael being lonely. It was something she had never associated with him. He was so self-assured, so confident, so *together,* that in many ways, he seemed invincible.

But he wasn't.

That day in his office with Jack Larsen, she had seen another side to Michael, a fish-out-of-water side. While Jeff would have been perfectly at ease sitting on the floor eating lunch, Michael had been reserved, to say the least. It had taken him some time to let down his guard, loosen his rock-hard control and warm up to the idea. In that time she had observed him.

This Michael was different from the one she had always known. There was a vulnerability to him, a man with a need. *Need* was something she could readily understand, and her heart had blossomed with the revelation, deepening the feelings she already had for him.

Once again, his mother's words came back to her: "He needs you, Johanna." She had thought that Arlene was making it up, dangling the phrase in front of her in an effort to convince her to take Michael up on his offer to work for him.

But there was a truth buried inside those words, one she now believed with all her heart. For all his money and cars and grand house in the country, Michael Ross was alone. By choice, she had no doubt, as there were a multitude of women out there who would kill for such a man. But, by choice or not, he had built a wall around himself.

And that was something she could relate to very well, for she had done the same. As long as that protective shell remained wrapped around her, she was safe from feeling too much, thinking too much, planning too much. Safe from all the insecurities she had lived with for so long.

Safe from falling head over heels in love with Michael Ross. Again.

But what was Michael's reason? What did Michael need protection from?

She shook her head, dismissing the questions. One step at a time, one day at a time seemed all she could handle right now. She nodded to the music, reaffirming her thoughts. It was right for her to go slow, she mused, as Michael's face flashed in her mind's eye. She *needed* to, now more than ever, and she was more than grateful for the luxury of letting herself just *be* herself for perhaps the first time in her life.

The music and her thoughts absorbed her, so much so that she didn't hear Michael's key in the front door, didn't see him enter the kitchen, didn't feel his presence as she let the rhythm of the music carry and control her.

He stood in the darkened doorway watching her, his hands on his hips, his navy blue suit jacket hanging open to reveal his blue-and-white-striped shirt and squiggly print tie. He was still perfectly groomed, like an alert executive ready to do battle at another round of meetings, instead of the bone-tired, quite possibly demonically possessed man that he really was.

Something had made him return home tonight.

He'd passed on the business dinner his client had arranged and canceled his hotel room. He'd caught a cab and taken the late shuttle out, driving straight home from the airport as if something had crooked a finger to him, beckoning him home, something urgent, important, something that couldn't—wouldn't—wait until tomorrow.

It hadn't been a sound in his head, but more a sensation throughout his body. During the return trip, the very air around him had been electric, thick and heavy with *something* he could almost but not quite smell with each breath he took—not a perfume exactly, but a scent that registered deep within his subconscious.

He'd followed it right to his front portico, felt it caress him as he entered, hearing the music even before he opened the door.

And there he discovered the source of his disturbance.

Johanna.

Billows of blue silk drifted out around her as she spun and swayed inside her own private world. Eyes shut, she hummed along as she sipped from the wine goblet. Her hair in disarray, her arms extended, she seemed a sprite, a siren, a dancing goddess in the throes of a magical chant.

The vision she made was a feast for his senses. Wild. Uninhibited. He followed her with his eyes. Her scent washed over him as she passed, and he breathed deeply. Clean. Fresh. Unadulterated woman.

His head spun, his mouth watered, his body tightened.

A smile creased his mouth as her voice, so charmingly off-key and earnest, seeped into him. She sipped the wine again, three tiny sips in a row, and he felt his mouth go dry, parched, oh so thirsty for a drop of the fruity liquid on his own lips, his own tongue, wanting a taste of it...wanting a taste of her.

Michael's heart began to pound in tandem with her movements. He pushed off the doorway and took a step forward, out of the shadows and into the flickering candlelight.

Johanna opened her eyes. And stopped dead in her tracks. Her heart skipped a beat, and her stomach flip-flopped. She felt caught, like a misbehaving child playing dress-up in the attic. The tip of her tongue sneaked out to lick her lips, tasting the wine and her own apprehension, as well.

For a long moment, Johanna stared at him. As she did, a strange calm rolled over her. Like a misty fog from the sea, it engulfed her, filling her ears with a roaring noise. Her senses peaked, and over the roar she became aware of the music playing, aware of the candlelight, aware of each breath she took.

Michael didn't say a word. He looked as perfectly groomed as a mannequin in a Macy's window and more intense than she had ever seen him. In contrast, Johanna felt so loose and mellow from the music and the wine, she wanted to bestow the same gift upon him, and had to fight an urge to slowly undress him, freeing him from the stifling constraints of his business attire.

Instead she undressed him with her eyes.

Slowly, her gaze passed over his face, lingering for a moment at his full bottom lip before continuing its journey to his neat collar and tie. Her eyes roamed lower, to his chest, the muscles of which strained against his fitted designer shirt. In her mind, she caressed those muscles with the palms of her hands.

She traveled lower still, to his waist. Slowly, she imagined herself insinuating her fingers inside his belted waistband, feeling the heat of his skin through the layers of fabric.

Johanna shut her eyes and let herself take this a step farther and trace the line of his zipper with her fingertips. Her hands twitched with the sensations her thoughts provoked as she imagined him growing hard beneath her hands. Swaying toward him, she could almost see his powerful response to her touch, could almost feel the strength of his thighs against her own as she pressed herself into him.

She breathed deeply, reveling in her own passionate world. She opened her eyes as she completed her mind game and reversed the process. Her gaze moved over his perfectly tailored body until her eyes languorously reached his face. The entire trip took only seconds, but it was one of the best vacations she could ever remember having.

Michael stood stone still, as if any movement on his part would break the spell. He could only guess at her thoughts, but if the brightness of her eyes was any indication, he was in deep trouble. As if she sensed his apprehension, Johanna smiled, a slow, completely spontaneous, utterly female smile that sent out a series of very specific invitations of which he was sure she had no conscious idea.

The look on her face was lazy and as intoxicating as a sloe gin fizz. Michael read it loud and clear and wondered how much of the message came from the wine and how much came from Johanna. If he had a brain in his head, he would say a quick good-night, make his excuses, turn around and head up to his room ... alone. It would be too easy to get caught up in what was going on here, too easy to give in to what she was so blatantly offering, too easy to give in to the magic of the night.

He should go now, before it was too late, before she reached out to him, before he touched her.

But when he tried to move, he couldn't. He felt as if his feet were nailed to the floor. It was already too late. Too late.

"You're home." Johanna heard herself speak, but her voice was hoarse and she hardly recognized it.

"Yes," he answered softly.

"Why?" she asked, knowing she shouldn't do this to him, but unable to help herself.

"I wanted to be home."

"Why?" she asked again.

Michael pinned her with his eyes. How far did she want to take this? "I missed you."

He said it so simply, so matter-of-factly, Johanna felt herself shake from the inside out. She hadn't expected him to say that. Or admit it. Even if it were so. Which she was sure it wasn't. She looked into his eyes; they seemed to challenge her to react to his words.

"Did you really?"

"Yes."

She took a sip of wine to cover her nervousness. And backed away. "I was listening to the music—" she waved her hand toward the stereo "—and dancing...."

"So I see."

"And drinking wine."

Michael raised his eyebrows. "How much wine?"

Johanna smiled. "Not too much." She ambled over to him, lifted the goblet and offered it to him. "Have a taste." When Michael didn't move, she coaxed. "It's very good."

He looked down at the wineglass teetering precariously in her hand between them. His gaze followed the line of delicate royal blue buttons on her robe up to her neck, then to her chin, her wine-moistened lips and, finally, her half-closed hazel eyes.

She was playing a dangerous game with him. He wondered if she knew how dangerous. The temptation to taste the wine, her lips, then every inch of her was real and so potent, he felt his body harden and pray for release.

Suddenly he knew what Adam must have felt like as Eve dangled the apple under his nose. . . .

He took a sip.

"Chardonnay," he said.

"Your favorite."

"Yes."

"Here," she said, thrusting the wineglass into his hand. "You have this one. I'll pour another."

Johanna lifted her robe in both fists and ran off into the kitchen. She took another goblet off the shelf and poured more wine. Her hands were shaking so hard she had to anchor the stem of the glass to the counter with one hand while she poured with the other.

Michael watched her take another long sip of wine. Her eyes met his over the rim, and she giggled, patting her lips with the back of her hand to suppress it. She lifted the glass and walked over to him.

She tilted her head and looked up at him, a silly, little-girl smile on her lips. "I'm glad you're back."

He smiled back. He couldn't help it. She was too adorable. "You look beautiful tonight, Johanna," he said.

"I . . . Oh, you mean the robe! It is pretty, isn't it?" she said as she held out one side of the robe and made a half curtsy. "Thank you, kind sir."

"You're welcome," he said.

His eyes were particularly brilliant tonight, she thought, and had to look away. Johanna swung around to the stereo. Placing her glass on the speaker, she took an inordinately long time to rewind the tape, needing to collect herself.

As much as she liked to pretend otherwise, she was caught off guard by his sudden presence. She hadn't expected to see him tonight and would not have dressed in this flimsy robe with nothing underneath if she had. She felt open, vulnerable. If nothing else, she had promised herself she wouldn't put herself in these types of situations again, such as surprising him while working out or at the pool table. But she hadn't counted on him surprising her.

And he had.

Now the question was, what to do about it? She could end it all very quickly, say good-night and rush off to bed. He wouldn't try to stop her, she knew, but the idea of going to her room didn't appeal to her one bit.

She could, of course, sit primly on the old, beat-up couch and initiate a friendly conversation with him. She could ask him about his trip and tell him about her class. But she didn't really want to do that, either.

Which left only one thing. She could allow nature to take its course. She could test him. Test herself.

She had never done that. She had never pushed this attraction to the limits. Michael had always left her in complete control, and she had been the one to back away each time.

What would happen if she didn't back away? What would happen if she pulled out all the feminine stops she knew and ran with it? What would Michael do? What did he want her to do?

And did she dare try to find out?

Michael watched her facial expression change from apprehension to determination. He wondered what she was planning next, not too sure he should stick around to find out. He was playing a volatile game here, one that could backfire on him, big-time. All those promises he'd made to himself were in danger of going up in smoke. Literally. He was burning up with a desire more than ten years in the making.

He'd noticed that the wine bottle was only half-full, which didn't bode well for the strength of her judgment right now. Not that his was anything to brag about if his mad dash back from Boston was any indication of his mental state.

No, the best course of action he could take would be to leave before she made a final decision.

"Johanna—"

"Aren't you uncomfortable?" she asked as she walked over to him.

"I—uh, no, I'm not. Why do you ask?"

Johanna reached up and loosened his tie. "Every time I see you dressed like this I want to do something about it."

"Like what?"

"Like undress you."

He looked at her. She smiled. Apparently she'd made her decision.

Michael stood still for her as she pulled the knot out of his tie, letting the two ends hang free. He gritted his teeth and didn't move as she unbuttoned the top button of his shirt, the second, then the third. He clenched his fists and ignored his brain's warning bells as she spread her hands inside his shirt, knowing he should stop her, but unable to fight a heavy lethargy that seemed to overcome him.

Her touch was feather-light and erotically innocent. It didn't seem to matter anymore if she was playing a game or not.

"Your heart is beating very fast," she said softly, splaying her palm against that spot on his chest.

"Yes."

Johanna tilted her head and graced him with a catlike smile. "So is mine." She took hold of both ends of his unknotted tie and pulled him with her as she took two steps backward. "Dance with me."

Michael put down his wineglass and allowed her to lead him to the center of the room. She opened her arms to him and, quite naturally, he wrapped her inside his embrace. She fit perfectly.

They danced to the thick, sensuous sounds of the saxophone. Johanna rested her head on his shoulder. One hand caressed the back of his neck, the other was laced with his. They moved together for the entire length of the song, speaking only with their bodies.

As the music ended, Johanna lifted her head. Michael looked down at her and cupped her face in his hands. His head descended slowly, giving her every opportunity in the world to pull away. She didn't, and he kissed her. Without preliminaries, he swept inside her mouth with his tongue. Without reservation, she joined him, pressing herself into his body as he deepened the kiss even more.

Johanna's head was spinning. The combination of the wine, the music and the man were too much for her. She reached around him, holding him tightly by the waist, anchoring her fingers in his belt buckle for support before she fell to the floor at his feet.

Michael moved his hands from her face to her shoulders, around her back to cup and knead the soft flesh of her bottom. The silky material of the robe slid against her skin, letting him know beyond the shadow of a doubt that she was completely naked underneath.

His body began to throb. This was what had called him. This was what he'd rushed home for. There was no right, no wrong, no reason. Only Johanna and how she made him feel. He cradled himself between her legs. Her body was accepting, willing, as pliant as putty in his hands, and she opened herself to him. He grabbed fistfuls of material and inch by inch he lifted the robe until it was no longer a barrier.

"I want you," he whispered in her ear.

Johanna moaned into his mouth as his hands touched her
bare skin. It was all the acceptance Michael needed. He spun
her around, lifting her off the ground and laying her down
onto her back on the old couch. Her robe was bunched up
around her neck as Michael released her. Johanna fought
the buttons, trying to get free of it. Finally succeeding, she
flung it wide open.

The look alone in Michael's eyes was reward enough for
her efforts.

"Johanna...you are so...perfect...so beautiful...." His
voice was whisper soft and almost awestruck.

Johanna sat up and pulled his shirt out of his trousers.
Without further incentive, Michael shrugged out of it, then
unbuckled his belt.

"Let me," Johanna said, and she slowly lowered his zipper.

Their eyes met a moment, questions asked and answered
in a heartbeat. When she reached inside the opening to caress him, Michael's eyes shut and his jaw clenched. She
watched him fight for control as she ran her fingers up and
down the rock-hard length of him. The look on his face and
the reaction of his body to her touch made her breath catch
in her throat. She had never been this aroused, this turned-
on, this hungry for a man.

"Kiss me," was all she said. It was all that was necessary.

Once again their mouths met, their tongues mated and
their eyes closed in ecstasy. As Michael leaned over her, the
tips of her nipples rubbed against his chest, the friction intense and gentle at the same time. Almost reverently he
touched her breasts, brushing her sensitive nipples with the
backs of his hands. And then his lips replaced his hands.
Like candy, she melted in his mouth. He suckled her slowly,
deeply, first one side then the other. Johanna arched her

back, reaching up to meet him halfway, unable to stop herself, wanting what he had to give, wanting more...wanting all of him.

Michael caressed her stomach, abdomen and lower still, until he reached her special spot. Johanna bucked as he touched her. She was so wet, so swollen with need, he thought he might lose what little self-control he possessed. He rubbed his thumb against her in short stroking motions until soft, mewing sounds emerged from her.

"Johanna," he whispered in her ear as he continued his sensuous assault. "Now..."

She was lost, gone, beyond thinking, only feeling, only wanting, only needing. "Yes, Michael. Oh, yes. Please..."

Needing no more incentive, Michael pulled back and stood. He extended his hand to her. "Not here. Let's go upstairs."

Johanna pushed up on her elbows. "Why not here?"

"Humor me," he said.

Johanna felt a chill that had nothing to do with the temperature of the room. She clutched the ends of the robe and brought them up around her. "Tell me why first."

Michael ran a hand through his hair. "You're killing the mood, Johanna."

"Humor me," she said.

Michael let out a long breath. "It's the couch."

"What about it?"

He shook his head imperceptibly. "You don't remember, do you?"

"Remember what?"

"The couch," he repeated.

"What about it?" she repeated.

"It belonged to my parents."

Johanna sat up, a puzzled look on her face. "Your parents? Is that why you kept it?"

"Not exactly. It has a certain sentimental value. It was their living room couch."

Her head felt a little fuzzy, but she tried to envision where this beat-up old couch had stood in his parent's old home. Slowly, the picture cleared, and with it came a realization, one that literally knocked the wind out of her. She looked down at the piece of furniture as if she were seeing it for the first time. She reached out and touched it gingerly.

"This couch... This is where we—"

"Yes."

"And that's why you won't..."

"Yes. We never talked about it, Johanna. Maybe it's time we did."

Like a morning fog dissipating under the heat of the sun, the passion between them faded to an almost painful ache. She looked up at him. Michael jammed his hands in his pockets, not bothering to rezip his pants or don his shirt.

Johanna stood to face him. Her body began to shake, and she wrapped the flimsy material of the robe more protectively around herself. She felt tears forming behind her eyes and knew she had to get away from him as quickly as possible or she was going to lose it.

She opened her mouth, wanting to say something to him, but couldn't for the life of her think of a single thing to say. She turned toward the stairs, suddenly wanting to hide behind the doors of her room.

Michael touched her arm to stop her. "I don't want to repeat the past, Johanna."

She stared at his hand on her arm until he dropped it. Her eyes burned, and her stomach was in knots. Without answering him, she turned and ran up the stairs.

Neither do I, Michael. Neither do I.

Seven

When Johanna awoke the next morning, she had such a raging headache it took her a moment to orient herself. Unfortunately, with realization came a wave of mortification the likes of which she had never felt before.

Yes, she had. Once before. And over her similar behavior on the same damned couch. Someone, she thought, should have the good sense to burn that thing.

Carefully she turned her head to the left and checked the clock. After ten. Michael would be long gone. Thank God for small gifts. Throwing back the covers was a huge effort, but she managed to lift herself off the bed without too much permanent damage. She shuffled her way into the bathroom and immediately downed two aspirin.

What she viewed in the mirror did not cheer her. She had swollen slits where her eyes should have been, but then crying did that to a person, and she certainly had experienced a major crying jag last night. It had been long. It had been loud. It had been pathetically self-pitying.

And she had earned every last sob.

Michael had knocked on her door repeatedly, but she'd steadfastly refused to unlock it. For a while there she thought he might break it down, but he didn't, which was just as well because that probably would have driven her into the bathroom, and she could just imagine what she would have looked like this morning if she had slept in the bathtub all night.

Dodging the stray articles of clothing that lay strewn about her room, she stopped only to pick up the discarded royal blue robe. It was still beautiful to her tender, tear-strained eyes, and she didn't blame it one bit for last night's debacle. She petted the silky material before smoothing it out on the bed to be cared for later.

Johanna donned her jeans and an old Grateful Dead T-shirt that had belonged to Jeff. It seemed right that she wear something of his. She felt particularly close to him right now, just as she had with the first "morning after" disaster with Michael. He had been there for her that day, being the friend she desperately needed, and strangely, his old shirt gave her some of the same comfort now.

There was, however, something different this time, and that something was *her*.

She had been devastated when Michael rejected her, so wiped out that being depressed seemed like something to strive for. But not so today. Today's Johanna was more in control, more angry at herself, and at Michael, too, for allowing the situation to happen the way it had. She was determined not to let her emotions rule her again.

This time, she told herself as she descended the stairs and entered the kitchen, she was prepared to fight. Fight the past. Fight Michael. Even fight herself if it turned out that she was, as she had suspected for a very long time, her own worst enemy.

She made a cup of instant coffee in the microwave. Sitting on the stool, she sipped the hot liquid and, for the first time in weeks, longed for a cigarette. Light filtered in from the French doors, and she wished she had a pair of sunglasses for her sore eyes to hide behind. She swiveled on the stool in an attempt to block the sun.

It was then that she saw it.

Or, rather, that she *didn't* see it.

The infamous couch was gone.

Cup in hand, she rose slowly and walked into the den. The half-melted votive candles were sitting where she left them last night. The stereo doors were still open, the Kenny G tape hanging out of the deck. Everything was as it had been the night before. Except that the wall where the couch had been was now an empty space.

Where was it?

Johanna ran down to the basement to check, then up the stairs to each of the rooms. No couch. Where could it be? Michael couldn't very well have carried it out on his back this morning on his way to work. Or could he?

And why would he get rid of it, just like that?

Mobilized with a mental energy that defied her physical stamina, she hurried through her housework then showered and dressed. It was her day to work in his office. She had convinced herself last night that she would never be able to deal with him today, and had made a decision not to go in. But she changed her mind. The answer to the mystery of the missing couch was too intriguing to wait for evening.

She grabbed a jacket on the way out. The air was autumn crisp and, though the sun was shining brightly, the wind had a distinct bite to it. The promise of winter was just around the corner. Johanna took a deep breath before set-

tling herself in the car. She didn't start the engine right away.
Instead, she leaned on the steering wheel, listening to her
inner voice and feeling the world around her.

She felt the need to collect herself before facing Michael.
She rolled down the car window and let the air hit her face.
The coolness made her skin tingle. She listened to the sounds
of the day—a car passing on the road, a bird chirping in the
tree, the wind blowing the brown, gold and red leaves off
their branches. She watched the leaves swirl around in con-
fusion before they came to rest on the ground.

All her senses cleared, including her sixth sense. It told her
that something more than the onset of winter was in the air.
A change was about to take place. A confrontation of some
sort. She and Michael were about to embark on a new phase
in their somewhat tumultuous relationship.

Starting the engine, she drove down the now-familiar
winding roads, feeling that she was truly back home for the
first time since her return.

Michael was in a meeting when she arrived at his office,
which didn't surprise her. The man spent his life in meetings.

Johanna helped the receptionist with her filing, then
worked with the bookkeeper on billing until the woman left
for lunch. She'd kept her eye on the conference room door,
but other than a short break where sandwiches were passed
through a minuscule crack in the door, the meeting continued long after it was time for her to leave for the day.

Johanna was ready to give up. She freshened up in the
ladies' room and lifted her coat out of the hall closet on the
way out. As she turned the corner to the reception area, she
viewed Michael in his familiar stance of hands on hips,
talking to his assistant at the door.

He looked perfectly fine, not the basket case of nerves
and insecurities she had been today. How did he do that?

How did he turn it off and on? How did he ever manage that icy self-control?

As he finished his conversation, he spotted her. Stopping dead in his tracks, he turned his face from her for a moment in thought—or perhaps exasperation—and jammed his hands into his pants pockets. He clenched his jaw, obviously collecting himself before turning back to look at her. A decision seemed to have been made because he walked over to her, took hold of her arm and escorted her without a word into the empty hallway by the coatroom.

"We have to talk," he said.

"I agree."

"When?"

"Tonight. At dinner."

He shook his head. "No, not at home. Let's go someplace."

"Where?"

"There's a little Italian restaurant called Basil's down the road from here on the right." He checked his watch. "Can you meet me in, say, an hour?"

"Sure."

"Fine," he said as he began to walk away. "I'll see you there."

"Michael."

He stopped and turned. "Yes?"

"What happened to the couch?"

"It's gone."

"I know that," she said. "Where did it go?"

"Goodwill. I called them first thing this morning. They were very accommodating and came right away."

"I didn't hear anything," she said.

He gave her a wry smile. "You were dead to the world this morning, Johanna."

"Yes. Well. Why?"

"Why?"

"Why did you get rid of it?"

Michael stared at her for a long moment. His eyes were a blinding, brilliant blue. "It's outlived its usefulness. Don't you agree?"

Johanna watched him walk away, her mouth agape. She couldn't have agreed more.

The restaurant was practically empty when she arrived. The hostess led her to a table by the window, but she didn't feel much like being in a fishbowl tonight, so she requested a booth in the corner. Something told her privacy was going to be an important ingredient in this dinner.

The waiter approached her, but she explained she was waiting for Michael. She checked her watch, then checked the door. She took little sips of water to keep herself busy, but handling the ice-filled glass only made her hands colder than they already were. She fidgeted, studied the room's Mediterranean decor three or four times and smiled at the waiter each time he caught her eye.

No doubt she looked as nervous as she was. Part of her wanted Michael to walk through the door right now, and the other part of her wanted to jump up, get in the car and drive. Far. All the way back to California.

"Hi."

Her frantic thoughts were interrupted by Michael, who rushed in, bringing a trail of cold air in his wake.

He had barely hit the seat when Johanna asked, "What do you want to talk about?"

"May I take my coat off first?" he asked.

Johanna shrugged. "I thought you had something urgent you wanted to say."

"Not quite that urgent," he said with a noncommittal look.

"Then what?" she asked again as the waiter wasted no time in coming over to the table with the menus.

"Can I get you a drink?" the waiter asked. "Or perhaps a glass of wine?"

Johanna waved him off. "No thank you. Just a cola. With a twist."

Michael grinned at her. "Make that two," he said to the waiter. "A little too much wine last night, Johanna?"

"A little too much *everything* last night, Michael."

"I tried to apologize," he said solemnly. "You wouldn't open the door.

Johanna buried her head in the oversize menu. "Let's order."

Michael shook his head and lifted his menu in front of him. He was still crazed over the entire incident. He never thought she'd take off like that over the stupid couch. All he could think of at the time was making love with her in his big, comfortable bed. He'd been so ready, and she'd been so willing. He still didn't completely understand what had possessed him to want to stop and go upstairs.

But his aversion to the couch had been real. While it held a certain sentimental value, he found that he didn't want a retake of ten years ago. He didn't want to have to look at the damn couch in the morning the way he had looked at it for ten years.

It was idiotic and probably juvenile, but he wanted a fresh start, a new beginning for them. It hadn't entered his mind that she wouldn't understand and agree. It had never dawned on him that in all the time she'd been living with him she didn't recognize the couch as being *the* couch.

He thought she knew.

He thought she accepted it.

He thought it didn't matter to her.

But then, how would he possibly know anything about what went on in her mind? They'd never talked about that night. They'd never even acknowledged that they had made love before. It was a subject more taboo than her marriage to Jeff—maybe *because* of her marriage to Jeff. Whatever the case, he was reacting to his own view of the event, not hers.

And apparently hers was quite different from his.

He had never seen a woman cry like that. He hadn't known there was that much water in the human body. He also hadn't known what to do. She'd locked the door and chased him away, and though she needed comfort, his instincts told him that he was the last person to provide her with it.

What had triggered all that emotion? Certainly not the memory of making love with him on his parents' couch. She'd never given him the slightest indication that she harbored any feelings about that night. He'd blamed himself for too many years for pushing her into a bad marriage with his brother, but now he wondered if that was so.

Did he push her, or did she willingly jump?

Why *did* she marry Jeff?

And if he asked her outright, would she tell him the truth?

That was his purpose for tonight—to get to the truth, to clear up the fuzzies in his head . . . to bury his ambivalence over her marriage to his brother, once and for all.

If they were going to have a prayer in heaven to go forward, they would have to clean up the debris from the past. And that would start with him and his perceptions of her relationship with Jeff.

The waiter brought the sodas, and they ordered their food. Johanna folded her hands in front of her schoolgirl-style and looked him in the eye.

"We've ordered," she said. "We've gotten our drinks." She pointed to the sodas. "So, let's talk."

"Yes. Let's."

"What do you want to talk about, Michael?"

"You. Me." He leaned forward, resting his elbows on the table. "Jeff."

Johanna felt her back stiffen. "This isn't about Jeff. It's about you and me."

"You and me and Jeff. It's all connected, Johanna. You know it, I know it, and if Jeff were still alive, he'd agree. The two of us have tiptoed around the subject for too long. It has always and will always be between us. What happened last night was inevitable."

Johanna took a deep breath and sighed. "What do you want to know about Jeff?"

"Why did you marry him, Johanna?"

She looked away from him. "Why do most people get married?"

"Because they love each other. Don't answer a question with a question. Unless you're saying you were so in love with Jeff, you couldn't help yourself. Is that it?"

"Michael . . ."

"Then why?"

"Jeff is gone. This is very hard for me to talk about. Especially with you."

"Why especially with me?"

"Because he was your brother."

"And you were his wife. And now you and I are getting involved. Don't argue," he said, raising his hand to stop her from interrupting. "You know it's true."

"We're not *getting* involved, Michael. We've always *been* involved."

Michael sat back. A smile creased his face. "I'm glad you brought that up. Finally."

"What, finally?"

"The couch—"

"Not that again—"

"No, let's talk about your problem with the couch and what happened on it. Ten years ago and last night. The truth, Johanna. Admit it. It's the same thing."

"No, it's not the same," she said. "It's very different. Ten years ago, I was a naive virgin with a crush a mile long."

"And last night . . . ?"

"Last night I was Johanna Ross, Jeff Ross's widow, and that's a fact I can't change. You want the truth, Michael? The truth is I don't have a problem with the couch. You do."

That shut him up. He took a deep breath and ran a hand through his hair. His eyes were blazing, and she knew she'd hit a nerve. She could go on. She could remind him that she wasn't the one who had saved the damned couch all these years. But she chose not to point out the obvious to him. Maybe if she didn't delve so deeply, neither would he.

The dinner arrived, and they sat back while the waiter served them. They ate in silence, neither looking at the other.

"You're right," Michael said finally. Johanna looked up at him. He was staring at her, and his eyes held a sadness she had not seen before. "I have the problem, not you," he continued. "I can't seem to come to terms with all of this." Michael smiled a slow, sad smile. "I loved my brother, Johanna. You may not believe that the way we fought and all, but we were very close when we were young. I'd do anything for him, even . . ."

"Even what, Michael?"

He shook his head. "Nothing."

"Tell me."

"There's nothing to tell."

"Yes, there is," she said, "I can see it in your eyes. Is it about me?" She paused. "It *is,* isn't it?"

"No."

"You want honesty from me, Michael. That works both ways. Tell me."

"There's no point."

"There's no point in my telling you about our marriage, either, but still you want to hear about it. Well, I want to hear about this."

He nodded, lifted the glass and took a sip of soda. "Okay. You asked for it." He slowly replaced the glass on the table. "But you're not going to like it."

"Go on."

"After you left my house the night of the block party, Jeff came home. We shared a room upstairs, if you remember, and for some reason he wanted to talk. He never did talk to me much after I won the scholarship. I knew it bothered him, so I didn't push. But that night he'd had a few beers and it loosened him up. He went on and on about the band and taking it on the road. And then he told me about you."

"Me? What about me?"

"That he was in love with you."

"What? That's impossible. Jeff and I were friends. Only friends."

"Not in his mind. He had his heart set on you." Michael pushed back and let the waiter clear the table.

"Coffee?" the waiter asked, and they both nodded.

Johanna felt as if a lead weight were resting on her stomach. She couldn't believe what Michael was saying, but she knew in her heart what the results of his conversation with Jeff had been. Yet, masochist that she was, she had to hear him say it.

"And . . ."

"I'm sure you can guess the rest. There was no way I could tell him what had just taken place between you and me. Not after he'd bared his soul for the first time in years. Instead I listened and tried to be there for him. I made a decision—"

"Blood is thicker than water."

"Yes."

"And the next morning you came to my house and told me you couldn't see me anymore," Johanna said matter-of-factly.

He looked at her. "Yes."

Unbidden tears formed in her eyes. She bit her lip to control them. "Just answer one question, Michael. Did you feel anything at all for me back then?"

"You know I did."

She shook her head. "No. I didn't know. I *don't* know. All I know is what you said that morning. All I know is that you were gone—"

"And Jeff was there."

"Yes. Jeff was there. For me."

"I have a lot of guilt about that, Johanna. It took me years to realize what had really happened. I'm sorry."

"It's a little late for that."

"Try to understand. He was my brother. You were a kid next door. I thought you'd get over it. Do you think I would have done what I did if I thought the two of you would run off and get married?"

She shook her head. "I don't know." She was hurt, confused, and though dredging up those emotions would serve no purpose, she couldn't help it. Part of her was still that young, hurt teenage girl.

Johanna closed her eyes and sat back, resting her head against the booth. God help her, but she hated him right now, hated him for telling her the truth.

"Haven't you ever done something you're not particularly proud of?" he asked. "Haven't you ever wished you could turn back the clock and get a second chance?"

A picture of Jeff the night of the accident flashed through her mind, the car keys dangling from his fingers— "Yes," she whispered.

How many times had she repeated those same words to herself? Could she really hold Michael responsible for his actions ten years ago, when she couldn't reconcile her own the night of Jeff's death? And could she ever tell him what really led to his brother's death? What would he think of her then?

Blood is thicker than water....

Johanna patted her lips with the cloth napkin. She grabbed her jacket in one hand and her purse in the other.

"Where are you going?" Michael asked.

"Home."

"Talk to me, Johanna."

"There's nothing more to say."

"Tell me you understand."

"I understand." She looked him in the eye. "More than you know."

When Johanna returned home, she went straight to her room. She undressed, put on a nightshirt and got into bed with her books. She had homework to do, and now was as good a time as any to get it done. It would also force her to concentrate on something other than her conversation with Michael.

Her instincts had been right. A confrontation did take place. But not the one she'd expected. All this time she'd thought it was she who had the problem. After all, she had carried a torch for Michael for years. She had been rejected by him. She had married his brother on the rebound. It

wasn't until tonight she realized that what was going on between them went beyond the sexual pull that seemed to
control them.

Michael had been troubled, too.

He said he wanted the truth, but she was afraid he wasn't
really prepared to hear it. The truth was he couldn't reconcile his feelings for her—his *wanting* her—with the fact that
she had been married to his brother.

Well, that *was* a problem, because she couldn't change the
past. She couldn't undo what had already been done. He
said Jeff was still there between them, but that wasn't entirely true. At least, not from her point of view.

Painful as it had been, she had buried Jeff, in her mind
and in her heart. Though she still carried guilt over the accident, Johanna knew deep down that she had done everything possible to make her marriage work. It hadn't. But she
had no regrets on that end.

So that part of her life was over. What she was feeling for
Michael was old and new at the same time. What it wasn't
was as murky as his feelings for her. She wanted him physically, definitely, but she wanted his love, too.

Could he say the same? He was fighting an unwinnable
war. All she had to do was look at him, kiss him, touch him,
and she could see and feel his body's reaction. He wanted to
make love with her, but something—or someone—was
holding him back. Was it Jeff? Or was it himself?

What did he see when he took her in his arms, when he
kissed her, when he touched her body and set it on fire? Did
he see Johanna, a woman he might come to love? Or did he
see Jeff hovering in the background?

And most important of all, was it possible for him to put
her marriage to his brother behind him?

She felt weary even thinking about it, for certainly there
could be no future for them if he couldn't separate the

woman she was today from the woman he thought of as his sister-in-law. What was done was done. She was Jeff's widow. No amount of talking about her marriage would change that.

It was up to Michael to change. It was up to Michael to come to terms with her and who she was today.

She sighed, put the book down and rubbed her temples. Who was she kidding? She couldn't study tonight. She could barely breathe without thinking about him. Her body still ached with want from last night. But desire would not be enough to sustain them. There had to be more.

Or there had to be nothing.

She heard his footsteps creak on the stairs before the knock came.

"Come in," she said.

Michael walked into the room. "Johanna—"

"I don't want to talk about Jeff anymore," she said, suddenly crystal clear on the tack she was going to take.

"Okay..."

"Isn't that what you came in here for?" she asked.

"Not exactly. There was a message on the machine. The furniture is going to be delivered tomorrow between nine and one."

"Oh."

"Can you be home for it?"

"Yes."

"Thanks." He turned to leave.

"Michael?"

"Hmm?"

"I meant what I said."

"About Jeff?" he asked.

"Yes. That part of my life is over."

Michael leaned a hand on the doorjamb, opened his mouth to say something, then changed his mind. Johanna felt his tension, but she didn't care. She had the strongest urge to leave this house tonight and was sure if she had anyplace to go, she'd do just that.

He pinned her with his eyes. "Maybe we'd better just call it a night," he said, pushing off the door to leave.

"Maybe we'd better do more than that," she said before she could stop herself. Michael paused and turned. His look was dangerous. She knew he was angry with her attitude, but she couldn't help herself. "Maybe," she continued, "we'd better go back to our original deal, and I'll be your housekeeper. No more, no less."

His face was a mask of self-control, and he took an inordinately long time to answer her. "That may not be as easy as it sounds."

"Maybe not, but it's the only way I can stay here."

He nodded slowly, his jaw tight, the line of his lips grim. "Okay. If that's what you want."

"That's what I want."

He shut the door behind him, and Johanna let out a breath she hadn't realized she'd been holding.

That, Michael, is about all I can handle.

Eight

Pure and simple, she was driving him crazy.

Michael acknowledged that her decision to return their relationship back to square one was sound. They couldn't go on as they had been, moving too fast, at times out of control, with no idea where it might all lead. The past was still a formidable barrier between them, and both of them harbored reservations about whether or not they could ever really put it all behind them.

But their talk had cleared the air somewhat, and he did feel a bit relieved that Johanna had been able to discuss their past so candidly. They had climbed one more step, reached a new level, which made him feel slightly more free around her. Thanks to the couch, she'd acknowledged what had happened between them, and, on a rational level, he was pleased with the outcome. The problem was, he wasn't the least bit rational where Johanna was concerned, and never had been.

With all the analysis going on, it was right for him to apply the same scrutiny to himself. In plain English, she turned him on. All the talking and rationalizing in the world wouldn't change that fact. The last few weeks had been hell. This ridiculous arrangement was wearing on him. He couldn't move around his house or his office without running into her or signs of her. It was as if the heavens were testing his mettle. He'd bump into her all the time, in all states of dress... or undress. It didn't matter. His hands itched to touch her, his arms ached to hold her, his body throbbed to possess hers.

And with each incident, his frustration steadily grew, until now it was a living, breathing entity that shared his space on a daily basis. He still craved her, still wanted to make love with her, and telling himself he shouldn't want to didn't do a damned thing to stop the feeling. He thought about it all the time, every waking moment, and then carried it over into his dreams. He was wound tight as a coiled spring and felt just as ready to pop.

Whatever spark had been ignited between them ten years ago may have been tamped down, deprived of the necessary fuel or nurturing to become a full-blown blaze... but it had only been smoldering, never really disappearing completely.

It was clear to him now why they'd kept each other at arm's length all these years. The trouble was that as much as he wanted to control it, he couldn't. The spark was not only still there, it had grown and matured—as they had grown and matured—into a raging desire, stronger and more powerful than ever.

Which made going back absolutely impossible. This "housekeeper" thing was a farce, and Michael was going stark raving mad. He had agreed to it because she'd seemed so adamant and determined.

He'd had a strong feeling when she proposed going back to their original relationship that if he'd pushed her, or argued with her about her decision, she would have fled from him. To where, he didn't know, but a real fear had gripped him that she was capable of picking up and taking off. And no matter how bad things were going, he couldn't abide the thought of her leaving him.

Michael refused to question why that disturbed him so. It made no sense, really. He'd lived with her as only a shadow in his life for a very long time. As analytical as he was, he wasn't prepared to peel back all the layers of feelings he had for her. It was easier to deal with the sexual pull that had always been between them, easier to explain his body's wants, desires, needs. But not his soul's.

Despite all his introspection, this old/new arrangement wasn't working. Couldn't she see they had passed the point of no return? They couldn't pretend anymore. They couldn't go back to where they'd been before they'd kissed each other, before they'd touched each other, no matter how hard they tried.

When Johanna came down this morning all sleepy-eyed and fuzzy in her warm-up suit and slippers, he'd wanted to lead her right back upstairs to bed and bury his face in her neck, touch that still-warm spot behind her ear with his lips, hold her body up against his and feel her melt into him.

Instead, he'd sat at the kitchen table, trying to concentrate on reading the sports page of the newspaper while she prepared pancakes. She wouldn't even look at him as she served breakfast, taking her own dish to the counter to eat away from him like some damned servant.

Michael was determined to put an end to this in whatever way he could. He felt like a pressure cooker was inside him building a slow but steady burst of steam.

"Johanna."

She looked up at him.

"Can we at least be civil to each other?"

"Certainly," she said.

"Please sit with me, then."

Slowly, almost reluctantly, Johanna rose with her plate in hand and joined him at the table.

Michael watched her pour syrup on her pancakes, then cut them into little pieces and eat. In silence, he chewed his own food with slow deliberation, never taking his eyes from her.

After several minutes, she looked up at him. "What is it?" she asked.

"What is what?"

"Why are you staring at me like that?"

"I'm not staring. I'm looking. Can't I look?"

Johanna shrugged and continued eating. "I thought you wanted something."

"I do."

"Oh. Is there something you'd like me to do today? Other than prepare for tonight's dinner, that is."

Jack and Donna Sue Larsen were scheduled to come for dinner tonight. As much as Michael had wanted this dinner to cinch what he felt was an almost done deal with Larsen's company, the atmosphere between him and Johanna was not the most conducive to entertaining.

Instead of spending the evening on business, he wanted time alone with her. He wanted to use this free weekend time to coax her out of this absurd arrangement.

Or, if that didn't work, he wanted to take her and shake some sense into her.

"No," he said with a calmness that defied his inner turmoil.

"Fine," she said as she rose and scraped the remaining morsels of food from her plate into the garbage. "If there is anything else you'd like me to do, please let me know."

"Mr. Ross."

Johanna turned to him. "What?"

His face was hard, his eyes blazing. He stood and walked over to her. Defiantly, he handed her his plate. "You forgot to call me 'Mr. Ross.' The paid help usually addresses the employer in a proper, respectful manner."

Johanna backed up into the sink. "Michael . . ."

His eyebrows raised. "Oh, it's 'Michael,' is it? You don't like 'Mr. Ross?' What is it, Johanna? Too formal?"

"Don't do this," she said.

She turned her back to him and placed his dish in the sink on top of hers. Her heart was pounding. Lifting the tap handle, she ran the water full blast and soaped the dishcloth. He was standing right behind her, his body not quite touching hers but close enough for her to feel his heat.

Johanna bit her lip. He was angry, and while part of her acknowledged that he had some right to be, she still wished he would leave her alone. She wasn't as strong as she looked. These past days of polite formality were torture for her, perhaps even more so than for him.

Like it or not, she was falling in love with him again. The more she tried to fight the feeling, the more it blindsided her. At odd times of the day or night. Even when he wasn't around. Like while she made his bed, folded his laundry, matched his socks. At times like these she would have to fight back tears of longing for something that could never be.

She felt his arms come around her waist as he pulled her against him. Her back stiffened, but she couldn't help herself from leaning into him. "Please, Michael . . ."

"Please what?" he whispered in her ear. "Please don't touch you? Please don't ache for you? I'm not as good at this as you. I can't pretend, Johanna. I can't wish it away. I want you."

"Right now?" She held up her soapy hands, trying to make light of his remark, despite the fact that her stomach was churning and her heart was beating fast and furious.

He reached up under her sweatshirt and cupped her free, full breasts in his hands. "Now. Later. Tonight. Tomorrow." His voice was hoarse and strained. "All the time."

He flicked the tips of his fingers against her nipples, and her sensitive peaks hardened into tiny pebbles. "Ah, Johanna, Johanna. I love the way your body responds to me." He ran a hand down over her belly, then into her waistband and below. He cupped her, finding her already hot and wet and wanting. He smiled against her ear. "Tell me the truth. Tell me you want me as much as I want you...."

Johanna gasped as he dipped his fingers into her, her body moving against his hand of its own accord. She rubbed her buttocks against his hard arousal, nestling him, massaging him, encouraging him.

He turned her around in his arms, wedging her between the sink and his body. She reached up and held his shoulders for support, her wet soapy hands leaving marks on his shirt in the process. Neither noticed or cared.

Her eyes were moist with emotion. "I can't very well deny it. I want you, too. But—"

He put a finger to her lips. "No buts. Not now. For once, no talking, no *thinking*. Just let it go. Just kiss me."

She did. Her lips parted, inviting him to plunder the sweetness that awaited him within. Michael feasted on her mouth with a hunger that defied reason, nibbling first her upper lip, then lower lip, until it all became too much and, at the same time, not nearly enough. He slanted his head and kissed her, his tongue sweeping inside, slowly exploring her inner recesses, losing himself in her addictive flavor.

Johanna gave up the fight. She ran her hands all over him, up his arms, around his back, down the hard lines of his thighs, as far as she could reach. But he had too many clothes on and she felt deprived. She pulled his shirt out of his pants, tearing at the bottom buttons in an effort to reach underneath to touch his broad chest and his stomach. His heart was beating hard and his skin was on fire, the dry heat radiating out to her, simultaneously warming her and sending chills down her spine.

She unfastened his pants, her fingers clumsy as they frantically fought with the fastening and zipper until she had managed to free him from the constraints of his clothing. He moaned into her mouth as her hand found him, hot, hard and smooth as velvet. She caressed him with long, firm strokes that fed the frenzy between them.

Michael pulled at her sweatpants until they passed over her hips and fell to below her knees. He cupped her bottom in his hands, kneading and separating the soft flesh as he lifted her almost off the floor. She spread her legs for him and, like radar, he unerringly found the center of her desire and nestled his arousal against her, poised, ready to make her his own.

But he didn't enter her. Instead, he slowly, steadily rubbed himself so close, but not quite into her, back and forth, back and forth against her petal-soft flesh. Johanna was wild with want and need. She urged him on, reaching down to touch him, to guide him into her, but he wouldn't have it, not yet, determined to drive her to the brink before he joined them together.

Johanna felt the kitchen floor tilt beneath her as her head began to spin. His lips left her mouth, trailing a line of wet kisses from her neck to her collarbone. He pulled at her sweatshirt, moving the material up around her neck to give him better access to her breasts. Taking one taut nipple into his mouth, he suckled her, a slow, bittersweet tug that corresponded with the ache in her belly.

She couldn't take any more. She had to have him. "Michael...please..."

He lifted her onto the edge of the sink. She shouted out his name as he thrust into her. He remained still for the longest moment, his breathing ragged. Johanna sighed into his hair, savoring the throbbing fullness within her.

She ran her fingers through his hair, and he raised his face to her. His look was loving, awestruck, and Johanna knew her face reflected the same. He began to move inside her, and she threw her head back, closing her eyes, freeing herself to feel each stroke of his body, each sensation, as they moved together.

The phone rang.

"Don't answer it," she begged.

She thrust her hips forward, taking him deeper into her body, and Michael responded in kind. Tiny beads of perspiration broke out on his forehead, and she combed his hair back from his forehead with her fingers, kissing his temples, his eyes, his cheeks, as their bodies danced to a perfect rhythm all their own.

The phone rang again.

"No..." he said, pulling out just enough to drive her crazy before joining them together again.

He kissed her, their mouths melding as tightly and perfectly as their bodies.

The phone rang for a third time.

He cupped her breasts and Johanna arched her back, using her hips to set a rhythm as sacred and old as time itself. This was what she'd dreamed of, fantasized about for longer than she could remember. She gave herself up to the feelings, so many, so diverse, she didn't know which to concentrate on first.

She was so lost in a world of her own that she didn't hear the answering machine kick in, didn't hear the voice speaking on the other end of the phone, didn't even realize something was wrong until Michael broke their kiss.

His body froze, and he jerked back from her.

Johanna followed his line of vision to the answering machine, and bewildered, disbelieving, they stared at it together.

"Just a reminder, children, that we will be leaving in two weeks for the cruise.... Johanna dear, Dad and I are so happy that you're with Michael. We know Jeff would have been so relieved ..."

"My God ..." Johanna said.

She shut her eyes tightly. His mother's voice went on with her message, dousing their ardor more effectively than a bucket of ice-cold water. Michael slowly released her legs, and in seemingly slow motion, Johanna slipped off the sink.

She adjusted her sweatsuit.

He rezipped his pants.

And then their eyes met.

Michael's chest was heaving as if he'd run a marathon. Johanna's face was flaming red.

As his mother's voice trailed off, the blaring sound of the last, long, shrill beep of the machine filled the room, taking with it the final vestiges of passion that had throbbed between them.

They stared at each other for a long time with the apprehension of two naughty children caught with their hands in the cookie jar. But their hands were not so innocent, and Johanna couldn't have felt more violated if Arlene had walked in on them making love. She felt herself begin to shake from the inside out and wondered what was going through Michael's mind.

"Talk to me, Johanna," Michael said.

She shook her head, her voice as paralyzed as her body.

Michael took a step toward her, and she cringed. "No," she pleaded.

Muttering an expletive, Michael grabbed his jacket off the back of the kitchen chair and he headed out of the room.

As she heard the front door slam, Johanna slumped against the counter. She brought her hand to her face and was surprised to find tears on her cheeks. She crumbled to the floor.

Michael's mother's words replayed in her head.

Just a reminder...

Yes, thank you, Arlene, she thought. A small but very effective reminder...of who and what they were to each other.

Michael entered the kitchen that evening with a hundred things on his mind and two words on his lips, but when he saw Johanna hovering over the stove, his mind went blank.

Even with her back to him, she looked fabulous. She was dressed in the black knit dress she'd bought on their shopping spree, and all the reasons he'd been against the purchase came back to him in full force. It was short. It was tight. It hugged her derriere with such tantalizing perfection that his hands involuntarily flexed at his sides as she bent over to open the oven door.

But he'd come in here to say he was sorry, to talk to her, to try to diffuse some of the discomfort they were feeling in each other's company after this morning's disastrous incident.

Leave it to Mom. Of all the times she might have chosen to call, she had picked the worst one possible. It had reminded him of when he was young. She'd shown up at the most inopportune times, as if she knew when he was up to something he shouldn't be. Mothers, he mused, may grow older, but they never lose their touch.

Not that he was blaming his mother. The fault was out-and-out his. Despite his best intentions, he couldn't seem to keep his hands still and his pants zipped whenever he was in the same room with Johanna. He'd been totally irresponsible and totally out of control. He cringed at the thought of the sordid picture he'd made—making love to her standing up in the kitchen, with no consideration and no protection of any kind.

Where was his brain?

Johanna wiggled her bottom as she basted the roast.

Don't answer that.

Johanna shut the oven door, rose and turned, her hands stuffed in two oven mitts, and a white chef's apron tied around her neck and waist. "Oh," she said, blushing as she spotted him by the doorway. "Dinner's almost ready."

Jack and Donna Sue Larsen were due to arrive soon. Johanna and Michael had taken turns getting ready. While she had showered, he set up the den. While he had dressed, she set the table and put the roast in the oven. That afternoon, she had made the hors d'oeuvres, and two trays were chilling in the refrigerator. She felt in control, or as in control as she could be with Michael around.

Then why were her hands shaking?

Michael had on a gray wool-blend suit, white shirt and black-and-red tie. He looked so handsome her stomach dropped. He also looked calm, cool, collected. Everything she wasn't. She'd lectured herself all afternoon, but apparently to no avail.

She wondered how she would be able to pull off the devoted sister-in-law-housekeeper act in front of their guests tonight. It was becoming increasingly more difficult to view herself in that way, and she knew she would spend a good part of this evening reminding herself of her official status in this house.

Not that the reminder they had received from Arlene earlier today hadn't shaken them both to the core.

By the time Michael had returned, there had been little time to talk, though he'd had that "We need to talk" look in his eye. But they were running late and that was fine with her. Besides, she knew what he would say if he'd had the chance. She could write the script herself. He'd tell her they had to be adult about this attraction. They had to control themselves and not put themselves into situations where they were vulnerable. They had to regain control.

For her sake. For his sake. For sanity's sake.

And Johanna would agree. The trouble was that all the talking in the world couldn't stop what she was feeling. Each day was more intense than the one before. She thought about him all the time, and she longed for him, for his lips, his touch.

When he had begun to make love to her this morning, when his body was joined with hers, her world had seemed complete, as if she'd come full circle. But the dream had been abruptly shattered, leaving her, in many ways, worse than before.

Now, instead of a ten-year-old memory, she'd had a taste of Michael, *the man*, which was surely more potent, but not enough to satisfy her. And all of a sudden, the perennially celibate Johanna Ross had a ravenous appetite for more.

"I'm sorry," he said, stuffing his hands in his pockets and making sure he stood ten feet away from her. "I was out of control this morning."

Johanna pulled off the mittens. "It wasn't all you, Michael. I didn't exactly push you away."

"I know that. But I initiated it. I took advantage." He paused. "It won't happen again."

She looked up at him. He had that determined look on his face. "What does that mean, Michael?"

"It means that if anything happens between us, it will be you who starts it, not me. Your choice."

"I don't understand."

"I've given this a lot of thought today, and I admit the problem is more mine than yours. The fact is I want you, Johanna, so badly I can't seem to control it. But we aren't two people who have just met and can let nature take its course. We have no way of knowing if anything can ever come of what's happening between us." He moved forward, reached out, but stopped short of touching distance. "But besides all that, I want you to know that I'm here for you...if you want me...if you need me."

"I see."

"Do you?"

"Yes, I think so," she said as she opened the refrigerator door with a calmness that defied the trembling she felt inside. She took out a tray of hors d'oeuvres and placed them on the counter. "Let me see. I want to get this straight." She rearranged the salmon mousse toast with the pepper and anchovy celery stalks, then looked up at him. "We can share your bed, have sex, but that's it. Nothing more. Do I have to return to my own room afterward?"

"That's not what I said—"

"Oh? Then how's this? We can share your bed, have sex and I'm allowed to stay the night. Occasionally. Is that more correct?"

"You're twisting my words—"

"No, I'm not," Johanna said, fire in her eyes. "What is this, Michael? Another offer to help poor, little Johanna? Not only food and shelter, but stud services, too?"

"My God, is that what you think? I thought you knew me better—

"I thought so, too."

The doorbell rang. Michael pointed his finger in her direction. "We'll continue this later," he said as he left to let the Larsens in.

Johanna stuck her tongue out at him as he left the room. Her choice, indeed! Who did he think he was? It was up to her to initiate it! As if she was love-starved and in desperate need of a man to satisfy her. Well, that part might have some validity to it, but *he* certainly didn't know that!

Or did he? Poor Johanna needed a man, and Michael, the ever-self-sacrificing brother-in-law, was perfectly willing to provide the service. This was beyond humiliating, it was downright insulting.

One thing about his offer she did accept, though. She needed to be in control. If he was going to stay put and let her lead the way, that was fine with her. She'd lived a happy, celibate life for quite a long time, and she could do it again. What she couldn't do was endure this roller coaster existence anymore.

And Michael had been right about going back. They were both wound too tight for that, but obviously he wasn't ready to take it to another level. If life consisted of just sex, Johanna was sure she and Michael would have it made. However, things were not so simple, and there were other feelings they had to sort out, especially the emotional issue of her marriage to Jeff.

No matter how hard they tried, they couldn't pretend that away. She still couldn't bring herself to talk about her marriage, and Michael never mentioned it, indicating to her that he preferred not to talk about his brother at all.

But talk or not, Jeff was there. It was as if she and Michael were able to look at each other, but only through a solid wall of glass. They could see each other, even long for each other, but were not emotionally ready to drop the barrier, to reach out and touch each other's true thoughts, true feelings. That was just too scary.

So, another talk to clear the air. For the time being. She wondered how long his resolve would last this time. He'd made a promise to her, but she had made that same promise to herself over and over again since her arrival. Johanna was beginning to feel that all they seemed to do was talk, promise, and then fall into each other's arms again.

There was a distinct pattern here of moving forward and retreating as if they were in battle. And maybe they were, she mused, as she heard voices of welcome in the hallway. But what they were fighting against was a ghost, and a past that couldn't be wished away. She untied her apron and hung it up on the hook before joining Michael to welcome their guests.

The furniture had arrived with little fanfare for what Johanna had felt was such a momentous occasion. Two years in the making, and the Ross house was suddenly a home. Johanna took a certain amount of pride in that. There was still a lot to do, of course, like accent pieces, pictures for the walls and whatnot, but compared to before, the place actually looked crowded.

Introductions were made, and drinks and hors d'oeuvres served in the den. Like Michael, Johanna considered this her favorite room. The earth tones, together with the teal and black geometric patterns of the couch and love seat, complemented the lamps and throw rug.

Michael had made a fire, and it was roaring at full speed as they sat to get acquainted.

"Jack tells me you're a widow, Johanna," Donna Sue said as she sipped a glass of wine.

"Yes, my husband was killed in a car accident."

"How awful," the older woman said.

Michael leaned forward and refilled Donna Sue's glass. "It was," he said. "A car hit him head-on. It had been stolen, and the driver abandoned it and took off. They never even found the guy. The police concluded from the empty beer cans in the car that he had been drunk."

"My goodness! How hard that must have been for you," she said to Johanna.

"Yes, it was very hard. But I'm all right now. Thanks to Michael." Johanna looked over to him, and their eyes met.

"A good man!" Jack said, slapping Michael on the back. "And a good *sales*man, too, I might add. I went over your presentation with some of my people and they were very impressed."

Michael turned his attention to Jack and the two men began to discuss business. Donna Sue pooh-poohed them with a wave of her hand.

"There he goes again," she said about her husband, then reached for a square of salmon toast as she looked around the den. "What a cozy room."

"Thank you," Johanna said. "Would you like to see the rest of the house?"

"I'd love to."

"Excuse us," Johanna said as she escorted Donna Sue upstairs.

She took Donna Sue to the rooms on the first and second levels, finishing off the tour on the top floor.

"This is just about the most darling house I've ever seen, Johanna," Donna Sue said as they made their way back down the stairs to join the men in the den.

"It still needs a lot of work," Johanna said. "Especially upstairs. You noticed that two of the bedrooms are completely empty."

"Well, y'all just got to fill them up with babies."

"That's up to Michael," Johanna said as noncommittally as possible, though her heart was thudding in her chest. "It's his house. I'm just his housekeeper."

Donna Sue waved her hand. "Oh, pooh. I've been watching that boy all night. He can't keep his eyes off you. He's got more in mind for you than housekeeping, if you ask me."

Johanna stopped her on the top step. "No, that's not true."

"Oh, it's true all right. I may be a country girl and a grandmother to boot, but Johanna, honey, that man is in *pain,*" Donna Sue said as she descended the stairs.

"Pain?" Johanna asked as she followed.

"Sure is. You got to put that boy out of his misery."

"I don't know what you mean," Johanna said.

Donna Sue patted her cheek and smiled. "Oh, I think you do. Give him what he wants, and maybe you'll find it's what you want, too."

"What's that wife of mine filling your ears with?" Jack's voice boomed out to them from the den.

Michael stood as the women entered the room. Johanna's face was a bright red, and he wondered what had happened upstairs.

"I was just giving Johanna here a piece of my mind," Donna Sue said to her husband.

"Now, sugar," Jack said, "don't you go embarrassing Johanna." He turned to Michael. "She does that, you know. Means well, but she's always giving advice where it's not asked for."

Michael grinned at Jack, then turned to Johanna. "Is dinner about ready?" he asked, and she nodded, grateful for the reprieve.

"Coming right up."

The meal was perfect. Johanna could almost feel her guests' approval radiating out to her. She couldn't help the burst of pride she felt at her accomplishment. She had never had the opportunity to give a formal dinner party before, and she hadn't been at all sure she had it in her. Her entertaining with Jeff had pretty much consisted of pizza and beer, but the look on Michael's face reaffirmed her own good feelings about tonight's success.

As the dessert was served and the evening came to an end, she felt she'd made a friend in Donna Sue Larsen. As she sipped her Darjeeling tea, Johanna let the woman's words wash over her.

Give him what he wants....

Donna Sue made it sound so simple...and maybe it was. Johanna glanced over at Michael. He was animated in his talk with Jack. He looked so boyish next to the older man, and her heart seemed to expand in her chest. She felt things for him she had never felt for another human being. She wanted him as much as he wanted her. Why was she so afraid to take the risk and give in to her feelings?

She'd have to think about that, she decided, and she tore her eyes away from him as Donna Sue offered to help clear the table.

Michael lifted his brandy and studied Johanna as Jack filled his ear with things he knew he should be paying attention to but couldn't for the life of him focus on. She looked so beautiful tonight, so soft and tempting, so perfectly right in this setting, he couldn't imagine his house—his life—without her.

"So how about next weekend?" Jack asked.

"Sounds good to me." Donna Sue added, "We'll be going home to Texas after that."

"Next weekend okay with you, Johanna?" Jack asked.

"That's up to Michael," she said.

"So what do you say, Ross? How's that sound?"

Michael shook his head, returning himself to the here and now. "How does what sound?"

Johanna looked over at him, her eyebrows arched in warning. "Jack and Donna Sue have invited us to spend a night next weekend as their guests in New York."

"Uh...next weekend?" he asked, stalling for time.

"Right," Jack said. "All my people will be in for our annual conference this week. I'd like you to meet my crew before we leave."

"We can go out to dinner afterward," Donna Sue said. "It would be easier if you stayed overnight. Any reason y'all can't make it?"

Michael looked over to Johanna. "Anything you can think of?"

Johanna gritted her teeth. "No. Not a thing."

"Then I guess we can—"

"Then it's settled," Jack said, pushing out his chair and slapping his thigh. "I'll have my people call you with the arrangements."

They took an inordinately long time to say their goodnights at the door. As the women exchanged phone numbers, Jack took him aside and nodded toward Johanna.

"She's sweet as could be, Ross," Jack said. "I wouldn't let her get away if I were you."

"I don't intend to," Michael said, realizing as soon as the words left his mouth that he meant it. He wanted Johanna in his life in some way, any way she'd allow. Michael glanced at her, and a poignant wave of longing gripped him.

"Good, good," Jack said as he slapped Michael's back. "Come on, Donna Sue, enough gabbing. It's time to go."

Johanna stood next to Michael and watched the two drive away before making a hasty retreat from his side. Michael locked up and checked the waning fire before helping Johanna clean up in the kitchen. They worked together side by side in silence. Johanna set the dishwasher and hung up her apron for the night.

"Thank you for a wonderful evening," he said.

"Only doing my job."

He grabbed hold of her wrist as she moved to leave the room. "About what you said earlier. That's not what I meant, Johanna. You can't think that—"

"Oh, Michael. I'm so confused, I don't know what to think anymore." She looked up at him. His eyes pinned her, holding her captive. "I need some time," she whispered.

"If you don't want to go next weekend, you don't have to. I'll call Jack and make your excuses."

"Do *you* want me to go?" she asked, feeling the heat of his touch, wanting more, but not knowing how to ask for it.

"It's up to you."

"That's not what I asked."

Michael dropped her wrist and gave her a long look. He walked over to the table. He shrugged out of his jacket and laid it across the back of the chair. Then he looked at her. "You know I do."

He said it so softly, Johanna felt it down to her toes. She swallowed. "Then I'll go."

She turned from him and made her way upstairs.

"Johanna . . . about this morning . . ."

"Yes?"

"We were both upset, and rightly so. My mother's voice put Jeff right there, between us. I've got to admit, it threw me."

"I know. Me too." she said.

"Trouble is, it's going to happen again."

"Oh, Michael, what are we going to do?"

He came to her and wrapped his arms around her, pulling her close to him. His scent drifted over her, and Johanna longed to give in to her desires and lean into him.

"We have to deal with it, Johanna. This isn't going to go away. I can't look at you, be with you and not want to touch you." He pulled back and their eyes met. "I made a promise today. I'm trying to be patient. It's not my greatest virtue, Johanna, but I'm going to do my best to give you the space you need." He let her go and she took a step back. "It's up to you," he said again.

Johanna retired for the night. Michael was true to his word. He didn't come near her, didn't follow her, didn't make any move toward her in any way. As she rested her head on her pillow, she heard his footsteps in the hallway. Her heart skipped a beat when he paused. She could almost *feel* his presence on the other side of her door, but instead of knocking, he moved on. She shut her eyes in disappointment and tried to squelch the pang of desire that had taken up residence in her belly.

Donna Sue's words came back once again to haunt her. *Give him what he wants. . . .*

"And what is that, Michael?" she whispered into the darkness of her room.

Sex? Definitely. Love? Maybe. But could she give him her body as she had when she was young, with no plan and no expectations? Could she settle again in her life for half the prize, as she had in her marriage to Jeff?

She wanted him, there was no question about that, but what kind of a future would they have if Jeff haunted every aspect of their lives?

"What do you want, Michael? What do *I* want?"

Perhaps next weekend she would find out.

Nine

Johanna was frazzled by the time she arrived at the posh Central Park South hotel where she was to meet Michael. Traffic had been a nightmare, and she had inched her way through the Lincoln Tunnel from New Jersey into New York. Exasperated, she checked her watch. Five forty-five. Michael's meeting with Jack was to end at six. Hurrying to check in, she breathed a sigh of relief when she found that he hadn't arrived yet.

She tipped the bellman and looked around. The suite was elegant with a magnificent view of the park, and Johanna couldn't help but be impressed. A huge vase filled with fresh flowers decorated the coffee table in the sitting area, and a bottle of champagne was chilling nearby. She read the welcome note from the Larsens and smiled, knowing the gesture had come from Donna Sue.

After the dinner party, Donna Sue had taken it upon herself to cluck over Johanna like a mother hen. She called almost every day, and though Michael felt she was a bit of a nuisance, Johanna kind of liked the attention. It had been a long time since she'd had that type of concern directed at her. The only bad part was Donna Sue's constant references to Johanna's relationship with Michael. Johanna knew she was only playing matchmaker, but her chatter about what beautiful babies they'd make only added to Johanna's anxiety, making it all the more difficult for her to put those impossible dreams out of her mind.

So she had to put on a good face and go out with the Larsens this weekend. She knew from little hints Donna Sue dropped in conversation that Jack was leaning heavily in Michael's favor on the new contract. She hoped this royal treatment was an indication that he had already made up his mind. It meant a lot to Michael, and Johanna wanted to do all she could to help him close this deal.

Even if it meant once again playing the ever-efficient business hostess.

Shrugging out of her jacket, Johanna kicked off her shoes and allowed herself a moment's relaxation. She ambled around the room, admiring the decor. The green-and-white floral pattern on the sofa matched the wallpaper perfectly, which extended right up and across the ceiling. She wiggled her toes into the thick hunter green carpeting as she checked out both bedrooms off to either side, too enamored with the place to make a choice just yet.

Instead, she pulled back the curtain from one of the windows and gazed out over the park. Well above the noise, Johanna leaned against the window frame and became wistful. She couldn't remember the last time she was in the city. Before she married Jeff, certainly, but the exact event eluded her.

There was something about New York that had always charmed and intrigued her, even as a young girl. The frantic pace of the traffic below and the hustle and bustle of the people contrasted drastically with the tranquil picture of the park. She glanced at the horses and hansom cabs that lined the curb. Some were decorated flamboyantly, others more traditional and subdued, but each, like the city itself, was delightfully unique. Not to mention custom-made for lovers.

She let go of the curtain, and it fell back into place. Johanna sighed. As much as she would have liked to pretend, this was not a romantic weekend in the city. This was business. Michael had more than once offered to let her off the hook and stay at home. She had been the one to insist. A deal was a deal, and he had kept his end of the bargain. School was going well, and the housekeeper salary he paid her was slowly but surely taking care of her debts. They may not have gone back to square one, but they had come close enough to make her feel she owed him this weekend.

Yet it left her with such a feeling of waste. The city, the suite, even the hassle of getting here, had all contributed to an anticipation she couldn't tamp down. In the past she could only dream of sharing such a time with Michael, and here it was, a reality. But the reality of it was too cut-and-dried to inspire anything but regret.

No matter how close they became, no matter how much they wanted each other, she feared that to Michael she would always be first and foremost Jeff's wife.

How could they have come so far and still be nowhere?

Johanna shook her head in an effort to snap herself out of her strange mood. Noticing her overnight bag, Johanna decided to unpack. She passed on the bigger master suite and opted for the smaller bedroom. Michael would probably protest when he arrived, wanting her to take the larger room with the more spectacular view, but if she insisted otherwise, he would soon acquiesce.

As he had seemed to do with *everything* she said or did this past week.

His willpower amazed her. More than once their eyes had met, held and spoken of things they couldn't seem to say to each other with words. His gaze seemed to follow her, lazily, longingly, but even the hooded slits of blue could not disguise the signs of his ever-present desire.

She'd come to know that look. It was the one he had right before he kissed her, and her heart fluttered in her chest each time she caught him staring at her in that way.

Yet he did nothing. If he was reading the newspaper, he'd turn the page. If he was passing through the room, he'd stop for the briefest moment, then move on. If he hesitated during his meal, he'd resume eating. And with each instance, her resolve would break down a little more.

Give him what he wants....

She flipped open her suitcase and shook out each item before hanging it in the closet. Her hand stilled when she came to the negligee Michael had bought her. Slowly, she caressed the material before picking it up, and when she did, the silk unfolded like a blue waterfall through her hands.

She'd purposely packed it to put pressure on herself. If there was ever going to be a time when she would wear it, when she would test the power of her femininity, it was here.

Maybe even tonight.

The thought sent her blood pulsing through her body. Her need for him was an almost tangible thing that clung to her like a heavy, wet, wool cloak. It pressed against her, always there, cloying, suffocating, with only one means of release.

But Michael had said it was up to her, and after his behavior this week, she had no doubt he'd meant it. While she wanted to call his bluff, take him up on his offer and be free of this need, she knew that with the freedom would come a price, one she still wasn't sure she was prepared to pay.

She shut her eyes. Was she strong enough to give her body to him, but hold tight and fast on to her heart? She already knew the answer to that....

Quickly, she hung the negligee in the closet. Out of sight, but not out of mind.

Not knowing what their evening plans called for, Johanna laid across the bed fully dressed. She ran her hand over the quilted bedspread, outlining the swirls and whorls in the design with her fingertips. She debated whether to take her shower first or a quick nap. Not that she would sleep a wink. She was too charged.

She was contemplating the night ahead when she heard Michael come in. Jumping up, she poked her head out of her bedroom door.

"Hi," she said. "How did it go?" He looked little-boy tired. She noticed his tie was loosened, and her fingers itched to pull on it as she had the night they'd danced, only this time she'd drag him into her room and—

"Very well," he said. "They seem like a great bunch of guys. I have a real good feeling about this."

"Are we on our own for tonight?" she asked hopefully.

Michael dropped his suitcase. "Not exactly. We're meeting Donna Sue and Jack for dinner. Which I understand will end fairly early. Jack's big meeting with all his people is in the morning, and I'm sure it won't be a late night." He took off his jacket and dropped it on the sofa. "This is some place," he said as he looked around.

Johanna came out of her room. "Check out the view."

As she held back the curtain, Michael glanced out quickly, more interested in her than Central Park. He couldn't believe how anxious he had been for the meeting to end so that he could get to the hotel to meet her. Each day was worse than the day before. Hurry and work. Finish up quickly. Get home to Johanna.

"Nice," he said.

"That's all you can say? Nice?"

"Great . . . terrific . . . beautiful."

He wasn't looking out the window. His eyes caressed her face, and he watched her blush. He wondered if his own look was as transparent. Desire gnawed at his belly day and night now, with no relief in sight. He had only himself to blame. He had set the impossible rules. He had given her the ultimate power over him.

The worst part was that he knew he could just as easily take it away. All he'd have to do was touch her, and she'd melt into him. The thought made him randy and hard. He daydreamed about doing that, of ending this charade, of making love with her once and for all, slowly, passionately, thoroughly, the way he'd always wanted but never seemed able to do.

She wouldn't complain or argue. Or stop him.

Which meant he had to stop himself.

He reached up and pushed a strand of hair behind her ear. She leaned into his palm and her soft, sweet scent drifted over him.

"Michael..."

Her voice was strained. Was it an invitation? he wondered... or a warning? Not sure—never sure anymore—he dropped his hand and took a step back.

Johanna's insides were trembling. Heaven help her, but she wanted him right here, right now. It embarrassed her to know that he could control himself while she could not. To hide her discomfort, Johanna let go of the curtain and moved past him to the center of the room.

"Any problems driving in?" Michael asked as if nothing had passed between them.

"Traffic was horrible," she said, amazed at the calmness of her voice, "but I made it unscathed." She paused. "I can't say the same for you. You look tired." Johanna dug her nails into her palm to stop herself from touching him.

"Yeah. Long day," he said, running a hand through his hair. "I need a quick shower before we go out to dinner."

"That's what I was about to do," Johanna said.

Michael stared at her for a long moment as the image took form: the two of them naked, bodies pressed against each other as they stood with the warm water of the shower washing over them, kissing, touching...more.

Don't start that again, he admonished himself. But warnings aside, he held himself in check, physically stopping himself from going to her, from taking her in his arms, from making that fleeting image a reality.

"Then we'd better get started. We're meeting them at a restaurant around the corner in about an hour," he said, heading in the opposite direction of the room she'd come out of. "This one mine?" he asked, and she nodded as he disappeared inside, leaving the door open. "I'm starved," he called out to her. "How about you?"

"Me too." *For you.*

"Be ready in a half hour?" he asked from the doorway as he pulled off his tie and unbuttoned his shirt.

"Sure."

She watched his door shut behind him, then she returned to her room as well. Her heart felt heavy as she picked out a dress to wear to dinner. Her throat clogged with emotion as she unpacked her toiletries in the bathroom. Why had he laid it all in her lap? Why did *she* have to be the one to make the decision?

The thoughts were too heavy, the dilemma too familiar, for her weary brain to sort through right now. She turned the water on full blast, gave up the fight and decided to let the night happen.

The restaurant was on the top floor of one of the highest buildings in midtown. Lights from the city shone in from every corner of the dining room. The view was breathtaking, the dinner gourmet and the company more than pleasant. Johanna and Michael sat across from the Larsens as the waiter poured each of them an after-dinner brandy. Jack waited for him to finish and walk away, then he lifted his glass.

"To Larsen, Inc., and Ross Marketing. May this be the beginning of a beautiful partnership." Jack brought his glass to his lips, but Michael hesitated. "Go ahead and drink up, Mike," Jack said. "You've got the account."

Johanna beamed with delight at Donna Sue, and Michael and Jack clinked glasses, sealing the deal.

"You won't be sorry," Michael said.

"I'm counting on that!" Jack laughed.

As the two men began to talk business, Donna Sue leaned over to Johanna. "Isn't that just like men?" she asked. "Have to ruin a perfectly fine meal with business talk. Let's take a walk to the powder room...."

Johanna followed the older woman into the rest room. As the door shut behind them, they primped in front of the mirror.

"Anything new?" Donna Sue asked as she applied her lipstick.

"With...?" Johanna asked as she ran a comb through her hair.

"You and Michael."

Johanna looked at her in the mirror. "Such as?"

"You know..."

Johanna shook her head. "No."

"Well, why ever not?"

"Donna Sue—"

"Now, you can tell me to mind my own business. It won't be the first time I've been told off, but I've gotta say what's on my mind. You and Michael look too good together. Any fool can see y'all are just made for each other. I can't stand to see you both so unhappy."

"We're not unhappy... and there's a lot more to it than just looking good together. There's... Well, there's a lot more, that's all." She was not about to discuss Jeff in the ladies' room.

"You remember what I told you?"

"Give him what he wants? Yes. I remember. But what happens when he doesn't *know* what he wants? What if what he wants is not enough for me? What do I do then?"

"Then give him what he *needs*." Donna Sue touched her shoulder. "The good Lord will take care of the rest."

The men stood when they returned to the table. The bill had already been paid, and they were ready to leave. The two couples walked back to the hotel together and said their goodbyes outside of the elevator.

"If we miss you in the morning, have a good trip back," Michael said to Jack as they shook hands.

"Keep in touch," Donna Sue called out as the elevator door closed, and Johanna smiled and waved her promise to do so.

"Nice people," Michael said.

"Very nice," she agreed. "And congratulations." She pushed up onto her tiptoes and kissed his cheek.

"Thanks," he said with a smile from ear to ear. "I wasn't really sure until tonight that he would go for the deal."

"You never gave any indication you were anything but confident. Overconfident, even," she said as they walked into the lobby.

He shrugged. "If that's what it takes."

"Always in control," she said.

He stopped in midstride and looked at her. His eyes were a brilliant blue. "Not always."

Johanna looked away and urged him forward. "Let's take a walk," she said, and they headed out of the hotel. She didn't want to ruin the warm feelings between them with endless talk that went nowhere. "Look." She pointed to the hansom cabs. "Ever since I was a very little girl, I've wanted to do that."

"Never have?"

"Uh-uh," she said.

"Come on. Let's do it."

"Are you sure?" she asked.

"I can't very well let you pass up this golden opportunity to fulfill a childhood dream, now can I?"

Johanna laughed out loud as he handed her up into the cab. They decided to let the driver have his way with them as they sat back into the plush seats, a blanket over their legs for warmth. They were close, but not touching. Johanna tilted her head to the side and leaned back against the cushions as the carriage rambled forward.

"This is fabulous," Johanna said, feeling like Cinderella in her pumpkin. She glanced at Michael. "Have you ever done this before?"

"Yes."

"With a date?"

"No, actually, with my family. When we were kids, my parents took Jeff and me for a ride." He laughed. "I can still remember it. My mother was a nervous wreck because Jeff insisted on riding up on top with the driver. He was jumping around so much I had to grab him. We *both* almost fell."

"He never did grow up," Johanna said. "If he were here now, he'd be up there with the driver again."

"Yeah," Michael said softly, "he would."

For a long moment they sat side by side in heavy silence, the clip-clop of the horse and the sounds of the city making it seem even more so.

"It must have been hard on you."

Johanna turned to him. "In what way?"

"Being the only adult in the relationship."

Johanna grinned. "Jeff was a challenge."

"That's what my mother and father used to say."

"But they loved him," she said.

"We all loved him, Johanna." He paused. "Even me. We argued about a lot of things, but I think he felt the same way."

"He did. He used to brag about you all the time."

"Really? I thought he hated the way I lived my life."

Johanna shrugged. "I think he covered up a lot. He respected what you did, all you accomplished. He couldn't measure up, so he rebelled."

"The classic sibling rivalry."

"Yes."

Michael turned to face her. "We should talk about him more often," he said softly.

"I didn't think you wanted to," she said. "I thought talking about Jeff made you uncomfortable."

"No." He paused. "I thought it made *you* uncomfortable."

They looked at each other and laughed.

"Come on over here," he said softly.

Johanna scooted over to him. Michael wrapped his arm around her and hugged her closely. She cuddled against his chest and he rested his chin on her head.

"You know, it would be great if Jeff had left us a will, a letter, or even a note telling us it was all right with him for us to be together." He kissed her hair. "But he didn't. So you and I are just going to have to figure this out on our own."

Johanna looked up at him, her eyes shining with love. "When you hold me like this, it all seems so simple. But when I'm alone, I get confused. I start thinking again."

"About Jeff?"

"Sometimes...."

"The accident?"

"No," she said quickly. "I'd rather remember the good things."

"Tell me some," he said.

Johanna took a deep breath. "He was my best friend. Did you know that? I think that was the hardest part of his dying. I'd lost my best friend."

"But he was your husband, too."

"Yes," she said with drawn-out hesitation, "but in many ways we were more like partners, friends..."

"But not lovers."

She pulled back to look at him. "Why do you say that?"

"Because it's true. Because you've told me so."

"I've never said—"

"Yes, you have." He reached for her hand, and slowly drew circles in her palm with his index finger. "Your body told me." He looked up at her, his eyes so blue they sparkled in the night. "I could *feel* it. When I was inside you."

His words made Johanna's stomach twist with the bittersweet pain of remembered pleasure. Did he have any idea how he looked to her right now? How she felt about him? She licked her lips. "I—I told you. It had been a long time."

He nodded. "I know. And that may be part of it. But call it chemistry or something else—we have it, Johanna. I've never found anything anywhere near it with anyone else. And I'm arrogant enough to think that neither have you."

Johanna bit her lip. How much did she want to admit to him? How much *more* power over her did she want to give him? "Truth?"

"Please."

"I didn't even know it existed...."

"Oh, Johanna, sweetheart ... you have no idea how that makes me feel."

"Tell me."

He leaned toward her, so close his breath fanned her face. "I'd rather show you."

He brushed his lips against hers with a slow, back-and-forth motion, their breaths moistening their mouths as he gently sucked her lower lip into his mouth. Johanna's head was swimming. She parted her lips, and he took full advantage, his tongue sweeping inside, staking its claim, making her his own.

Michael had never remembered wanting a woman the way he wanted Johanna right now. His body, his mind, his soul was so tied up in her, he couldn't think of anything else. Jeff seemed a dim shadow, somewhere in the background, but no longer threatening, no longer vitally important. Surely she could feel it, too.

He ran his hand inside her coat, touching her breast through the material of her dress, feeling her nipple harden in response. She was so in tune with him, so perfect, his body throbbed to possess her completely, fully, totally.

Johanna leaned into him, and Michael lifted her across his lap. He drew the blanket up, wrapping them inside a private cocoon against the cool night air and the eyes of the world. Her skirt rode up, and he ran a hand up the inside of her thigh, caressing the soft skin beneath the silky hose. His touch was feather-light, but potent enough to send shivers up Johanna's spine. She closed her legs, trapping his hand between her thighs.

Reaching between them, she loosened his tie and unbuttoned his shirt. She felt his eyes on her as she caressed the soft tufts of hair that peaked out of the top of his shirt. Replacing her fingers with her lips, Johanna nuzzled him, kissing, nipping his neck as she worked her way down to his chest.

She felt him shudder beneath her mouth, the beat of his heart accelerating as she slid her hand from his lap to between his knees. Her hands felt their way to his belt, and with precision that belied her awkward position, she had it unbuckled in seconds. Her tongue touched the tight skin of his nipple at the same moment her hand found him.

Michael froze. "Johanna..." he whispered in warning, pulling at the blanket, insuring that they were covered in a cloak of privacy.

She knew where she was and what she was doing. Johanna didn't care. She continued to stroke him, wanting more than anything to please him the way he had pleased her so many times.

More. She wanted to taste him.

Divining her thoughts, Michael reached down and stopped her.

"Let me...."

He shook his head. "No...not here."

"Yes. Here. Now. I want to."

She resisted, but was no match for his strength as he pulled her up to face him. His voice was soft, but determined. "Johanna...I want to make love with you. All of you. In every way. Do you understand?"

"Yes..."

"But not here, not now. I want you in my bed, naked, private, without any chance of interruption." He cupped her face in his hands. "And then, my sweetheart, I am going to love you the way you've never been loved before."

Johanna felt the tears threaten behind her eyes. "Oh, Michael..."

"Tell me you want it too. Tell me you'll come to me. Willingly. Because you want *me*."

"Yes...only you."

She felt his hands tremble against her shoulders as the words left her lips. Michael shut his eyes and rested his forehead against hers and held her still for a long moment. When he opened his eyes, they were blazing.

"Let's go back to the room."

Johanna was dimly aware of the lights of Tavern-on-the-Green glittering in the distance as they rounded a curve in the road. She was too busy being mesmerized by the look, the promise in Michael's eyes. She sank against him, giving up whatever fight she had been waging, though for the life of her right now she couldn't remember what it was or why she'd seemed so intent on engaging in it.

Michael called out to the driver to return to the hotel. The driver snapped his whip in the air, urging the horses to pick up their pace. Michael held her tightly to him, but he didn't speak. Or think. To him, the time for that was over. He wanted her; she wanted him. The hell with the rest of it.

It seemed to take forever for the cab to return to its spot by the park. Michael helped her down, and together they walked across the street to the hotel and waited for the elevator.

Michael stood away from her, touching her only with his eyes. It was enough. Her insides were melting down with want for him, and she cursed each stop the elevator made that kept them from their own personal meeting with destiny. By the time the elevator arrived at their floor, she was shaking.

When they stepped into the suite, Michael turned and locked the doors. Johanna stood in the middle of the sitting room, her anticipation at a fever pitch as she waited for him to come to her, to take her in his arms, to take her to his bed....

He didn't. Instead, he walked past her, discarding his jacket, shirt and tie along the way. He stopped at his bedroom door and turned to her. "Johanna..."

Her stomach dropped. "Yes?"

"Come to me." And then he disappeared into his room, taking with him the magic of the moment, leaving her to once again make the decision ... alone.

It's up to you.

It was late, and the moon was high. Johanna sat on the edge of her bed, looking out over the park. The streets were quiet now, the traffic all but gone with only a rare pedestrian braving the night and the city. She tangled her fingers in the soft fabric of the blue negligee, caressing the silk as she deliberated her fate.

It's up to you.... Give him what he needs....

The thoughts whirled through her brain. He had done it to her again, dropping it all back in her lap, forcing her to make the decision. But was Michael offering himself to her with no strings attached? Sex with no love and even less future?

As from the first, she had no idea what was going on in his mind. He kept that wall intact throughout everything they'd been through. But no matter how cool and controlled he could be, she didn't believe for one minute that he was as uninvolved as he pretended. He couldn't kiss her the way he did, touch her the way he did, without feeling something. That might have been true the first time on his parents' couch when they were kids, but not anymore. He was a grown man now, with desires as powerful and all-consuming as her own.

Like it or not, Jeff's wife or not, she *was* part of his life now, and he needed her. Not just to take care of his house and work in his office, either. He needed her emotionally, as well.

She stood.

Come to me. . . .

All right, Michael Ross, I'll call your bluff, I'll take the first step.

She was shaking as she walked out of her room, scared to death of being hurt again. Inside, she knew that this time would be much, much worse. But it was time to make a move, to take the risk, to jump in headfirst. In her heart she knew it was what Jeff would tell her to do. And she was willing to bet her future that she was right.

She stopped in the sitting area. The dark soothed and protected her. She could turn around at any moment and retreat. No one would know. She felt herself trembling once again with indecision. But the alternative to moving forward was going back . . . and that was *nowhere,* a place she distinctly did not want to be.

Her resolve fortified her. She straightened her backbone and forced her feet to move. She placed her hand on the doorknob to his room, gripped it tightly, then turned it. It opened with the tiniest of sounds, and she stepped inside.

The click alerted him.

Eyes closed, Michael sensed her presence. Without moving, he opened his eyes and followed her progress as she seemed to glide toward him. He watched, waited, to see what she was about to do. She hesitated for a long moment, as if assessing the possibility that he was awake, then she proceeded once more.

The relief in his chest was palpable. Up until this moment, he hadn't been sure she would come to him. It had been a risk, calculated perhaps, but there had still been enough of a chance that she wouldn't be able to make the first move.

And it was so vitally important to him that she do that. He had to know that she wanted him, consciously wanted *him,* not some sexual substitute, not someone to satisfy her long-denied needs. She had to face the truth, whatever it was, and he had to take the chance that she might not be able to.

Or that the truth might not include him.

Every pore on his body went on red alert and tingled with anticipation. His heart was thudding so loudly in his chest, he could barely concentrate on the other sounds in the room—her breathing, the rustling sound of her nightgown against her legs, her footsteps gently creaking on the thick carpeting. His body tightened with each step she took, until he was hard. Rock hard.

He sat up.

She stopped dead in her tracks.

The moonlight filtered through the thin, white, voile curtains, providing Michael with just enough light to discern her outline. He blinked to adjust his eyes to the vision she made in the form-fitting blue negligee. She had done what he'd begun to feel was impossible. She had come to him, just as he'd asked. He felt as if he'd been dropped headfirst into the midst of a lifelong erotic dream, so real and terrifying was this fantasy come true.

An errant strap slid off her shoulder, exposing the top of one creamy breast, and he followed its descent with his eyes. Slowly, she pushed it back into place, her hand remaining in place across her breast in an unconscious protective gesture. It signaled her nervousness, and a wave of tenderness washed over him, so potent, so powerful, he thought his chest would burst from it.

Their eyes met. Michael lifted back the covers in silent invitation. He was naked, and Johanna hesitated for the briefest moment before slipping into bed beside him.

They didn't touch. Michael rested on his elbow facing her, and Johanna did the same. His eyes roamed her face, stopping at each feature, one by one, until they came to rest at her tremulous lips.

"Johanna . . . I didn't think you'd come."

"You had to know I would."

He shook his head. "No, I wasn't sure, not until this moment."

Johanna's heart twisted with his revelation. She touched his face with the palm of her hand. "Kiss me."

He did. Without touching her with his hands, Michael slanted his head toward hers and took her mouth whole with a hunger that was years in the making. This was no gentle kiss. There was no coaxing, no play. This was an already-there kiss, the kind of kiss lovers shared when their bodies were joined in the throes of passion.

Johanna was more than ready for whatever he had to offer. His mouth was hot and wet and commanding, and she whimpered as his tongue swept deep inside. She opened her mouth wider for him, kissing him back with all the love she had kept hidden for so long. Michael needed no further incentive. He pushed her back against the full down pillows and cupped her face in his hands.

Johanna reached up and ran her nails against his bare chest as he peeled down the straps of her nightgown, first one side, then the other.

Michael pulled back. Johanna's mouth was swollen, and she was short of breath. She watched him catch his index finger in the sweetheart V of the neckline and tug it down, releasing her breasts from their silken hiding place. His gaze swept over her, and Johanna opened herself to him, wound so tight and wanting so much, her insides melting in sweet surrender like maple syrup over hotcakes.

For a long moment, he only caressed her with his eyes, then ever so gently he smoothed his fingertips across the tops of her breasts to her sensitive nipples until they were hardened peaks.

He took one tender morsel into his mouth, suckling her slowly, stopping at intervals to blow cool air against the fevered peak before moving on to pay similar homage to the other side, then back again.

Johanna was crazed, her hips undulating with the movements of his mouth. As if he knew what she wanted, Michael slipped the nightgown farther down, exposing the gentle curve of her belly as he tasted his way down her body with hot, wet, openmouthed tiger kisses.

And then he sat back. Johanna opened her eyes to question him, but stopped cold. This was a Michael she had never seen before. His face was taut and tight with desire. He was all male, completely aroused and thoroughly in command. With a twist of his wrist, he flung the covers off them. Her heart fluttered in her chest as her nightgown followed the same flight pattern.

And then he moved over her....

She felt a moment's apprehension as he ran his hands up her inner thighs and spread her legs.

Michael sensed it, and he looked into her eyes to reassure her. "I want all of you, Johanna...in every way. Do you understand?"

"Yes," she said on a breath and a prayer.

She watched as he hovered over her. Then she shut her eyes, giving herself up to sensation as his body skimmed across hers. Up and down, back and forth, before he settled himself exactly where he wanted to be.

He began with light feather kisses, which he placed on the backs of her knees as he bent first one leg, then the other. He continued his assault with tiny, tip-of-the-tongue kisses as he licked his way up the insides of each thigh. And he completed his journey with his mouth on the center of her desire, in a kiss so complete, so intimate, she thought she might never take air into her lungs again. But dead or not, as his tongue worked its magic on her, she knew that this side of heaven had never been so near.

Michael didn't hesitate, or falter, or stop, but kept at her with a slow, steady pace that was driving her wild. Her body was moving forward at a fevered speed toward that special place she knew existed and wanted more than anything to visit again. She let herself go, gave herself up to the pleasure and concentrated only on Michael and the magic of his mouth.

Johanna's head was spinning. She reached down and threaded her fingers through Michael's hair, anchoring herself to him, knowing that if she didn't, she would surely fall off the edge of the earth.

And then it hit her, wave after beautiful wave of pure pleasure. Johanna called out his name, a lone, soulful moan that sounded as if she were in pain instead of in the throes of the most ultimate climax she had ever experienced.

Michael had to disentangle her fingers from his hair before she tore it out from the roots. He rested his chin on her belly and looked up at her, a thoroughly proud-as-a-peacock male look on his face.

Johanna pushed herself up on her elbows to view him. "You look quite pleased with yourself," she said.

"I'm pleased that you're pleased," he said as he nipped at her belly. "You *are* pleased, aren't you?"

"Oh, yes...."

He lifted himself up and braced his weight against his palms, one hand on each side of her. Muscles straining, he leaned forward, his face inches from hers. His eyes were so blue, they shone like beacons in the moonlight. "I want you, Johanna, so much."

She touched his face with her fingertips as he captured her mouth in a deep soul kiss. Johanna tasted herself on his lips, and again passion ignited between them, hotter and more intense than before.

He pushed her down into the softness of the pillows and feasted on her. She ran her hands over his chest, his back, his thighs, until she could stand it no more. Reaching between them, she took him in her hand. A groan escaped his lips. He broke the kiss and buried his face in her neck.

"Johanna, if...you...don't...stop...I'll..."

She stopped.

He turned his head and looked at her. "Come to *me*, Michael," she said, so softly he had to strain his ears to hear her. "Right here," she said, guiding him with her hand to the center of her desire.

Michael felt himself swell thicker and harder than he ever had before, as her warmth, her heat caressed him. He leaned over her and took a condom off the nightstand.

"Prepared, Michael?"

"Hopeful, Johanna."

She took the packet out of his hand. "May I?"

"Please...."

Michael shut his eyes as she protected him in a most thorough and imaginative way. And then he could wait no more. He nestled himself between her legs, poised and ready to make them one. His mind told him to go slow, take his time, not to frighten her, but his body was on fire, and he was beyond the point of reason. With one purposeful thrust, he joined them together.

"Oh, Michael..."

She arched up to meet him, each slow, sure stroke bringing her a little closer to him in every way possible. She told him she loved him with each movement of her body as she took him deeper and more fully inside her. As his pace grew more rapid, Johanna smiled, knowing she was pleasing him as much as he had pleased her. And then he reached between them, touching her, rubbing her with the pad of his finger, until she, too, was lost in a world of joyful sensation.

The explosion, when it came, was a white-hot flash that ran through them like lightning through a metal rod. Michael held her to him for a long time, absorbing the aftershocks. He rolled to his side, his arms steadfast and secure around her.

But his insides were shaking.

He shut his eyes and tried to catch his breath. He needed to reorient himself. Never had he lost himself so completely in a woman. Never had it been this good, this complete. Never had it been this . . . loving.

Johanna kissed his chest, and he let go of her enough to give her breathing room. She had a smile on her face, but when she looked up at him, he was frowning.

"Are you okay?" she asked.

"Hmm? Oh, yes. I'm fine. Fine."

But he didn't look fine. He looked troubled, and Johanna felt her stomach drop. How could it have been so wonderful for her and not for him?

She extricated herself from his embrace. "I-I'd better go. . . ."

He grabbed her wrist before she could get out of the bed. "Go where?"

"To my room?"

"No."

She shook her head. "No?"

"No."

"You want me to stay and sleep with you?" she asked.

Michael grinned and pulled her to him. "Well, let's just say I want you to stay. I'll make no promises about the 'sleeping' part. . . ."

Ten

Sunlight filtered through the flimsy curtains as Johanna and Michael lay in bed face-to-face. She felt an afterglow all over her as she outlined his features one by one with her fingertips. His eyes were ringed from lack of sleep, as, she had no doubt, were hers. But then, they hadn't done much more than doze in between some very passionate and highly erotic lovemaking throughout the night.

A small smile creased her lips at the thought. "People don't make love like this all the time, do they?" Johanna asked.

Michael brushed a strand of hair away from Johanna's face and anchored it behind her ear. "No." He grinned. "If they did, they'd die."

She laughed, and Michael leaned over to kiss her. She opened her mouth for him, knowing exactly what he liked and how he liked it.

"Mmm," he murmured against her mouth. "You taste so good."

"Are you as hungry as I am?" she asked.

"For food?"

She gave him a playful slap. "Yes, for food."

"As a matter of fact, I am. You put me through a hell of a workout last night—"

"*I* put *you* through...!"

"Look," he said, pointing to his shoulder. "Bite marks."

She examined the spot, then rubbed it with her finger. "They are not."

"Yes, they are. See? Perfect little dots. A regular little tigress in bed."

Johanna blushed. "I'm sorry...."

"Don't be." He planted a kiss on the tip of her nose. "I loved every minute of it."

"Me too."

They kissed again, this time a longer, more luxurious kiss, a practiced lover's kiss filled with the promise of passion.

"Feed me, woman!" he said before hopping up out of bed and heading for the shower.

"What do you want?" she called out. He stuck his head out from behind the bathroom door and wiggled his eyebrows like a dirty old man. She shook her head at him in warning. "I'll order some omelets.

"Omelets. How unromantic," he said.

"That all depends on how you serve them. And where." Michael stared at her, a bit bemused. Johanna thought he might even be blushing just a tiny bit. She smiled. "Go take your shower, Michael."

Not leaving the bed, she lifted the receiver and called room service with their breakfast order. Johanna stretched under the covers, feeling joyously sore in some very new and interesting spots, places she hadn't known she'd owned until last night.

The sound of the water running and the city outside drifted over her. She felt very pleased with herself. After all her indecision, after all her soul-searching, she had gone with her instincts. Last night had fulfilled every fantasy she'd ever had about Michael Ross—and a few she hadn't.

She couldn't remember being this happy, this content, and part of her wondered why had she waited so long. Even if this joy were only to last for a short time, she could feed on the memory of it for the rest of her life.

"Johanna!"

"Yes?"

"Come in here! Quick!"

She jumped out of bed and ran naked into the bathroom. "What is it?" she asked, poking her head inside the shower curtain.

She shrieked as Michael reached out and wrapped an arm around her waist. He lifted her into the tub.

"This," he said, and he kissed her deeply. "And this—" He ran his hands over her body. "And this..." He nipped an earlobe as he cupped her bottom and rubbed a hair-roughened thigh between her silky legs.

Johanna kissed his chest, his shoulder, the muscles of his arm as the warm water cascaded down over them. Michael massaged the wetness into her back, moving lower and lower still until his fingers reached their goal, touching her intimately, lovingly, and so thoroughly, she thought she'd melt with pleasure.

"I missed you," he said between kisses.

"No wonder. It's been a whole five minutes."

Johanna reached for the bar of soap and rubbed it into the middle of his chest, creating a soft lather. Then she ran

her fingers through it, washing and caressing him at the
same time.

"Too long."

Michael slanted his head and took her mouth. Their
tongues met, mated and danced to a rhythm they had practiced well the night before. She felt him stir against her and
deepened the kiss, opening her mouth farther, allowing
herself to be devoured by him.

He turned her around, and Johanna looked over her
shoulder to question him.

"Trust me," he said softly.

She needed no more than that. She willingly turned,
leaning her palms against the tiles, their coolness soothing
her heated skin. Michael's arms came around her as he
cupped her breasts in both hands, flicking her sensitive nipples with his fingers as he pressed himself against her.

He was fully aroused and Johanna opened herself to him,
loving him, trusting him, wanting him so much she couldn't
control her response to his need. Michael entered her slowly,
joining them together a bit at a time, moving with her, in
her, until her body accommodated him, until they were totally one.

Michael wrapped his arms around her waist, holding her
tightly to him, unable to move, only to savor the electric
shock of feelings that were bombarding his body at every
turn. She hugged him like a glove, so perfect in every way,
his mind had to do conscious battle with his body for control.

Johanna had never felt this possessed by a man, this
filled, this complete. She squirmed against him, lifting her
hips, urging him to move, wanting him to bring her to that
ultimate fulfillment she craved.

He didn't disappoint her. His hand slipped between her
legs and gently rubbed her special spot in tandem with the

thrust of his hips. With slow deliberation, he continued his assault on her senses. She shut her eyes, weak with need . . . and so close, so very close to her ultimate destination, she shook with anticipation.

"Oh, Michael. . . ." Johanna moaned his name out loud as the first wave hit her.

She leaned her face against the tiles, anchoring herself for the onslaught of spasm after spasm of pleasure.

It was all too much for Michael. Her body was in control, pulling his along with her. With one final thrust he gave up the battle and found himself in a world too bright and explosive to be real.

As he drifted down to earth, he leaned forward and buried his face in her neck, singing her praises in murmured words for her ears alone.

The water revived them, and in silence, Johanna turned in his arms. She reached up and clasped her hands around his neck. Michael kissed her, a long, thorough kiss that held such a poignant promise, her stomach twisted with love for him, a love that had never really gone away, only grown and intensified over the years.

When she looked into his eyes, his gaze was a blue so brilliant, so penetrating and so loving, she couldn't stop the eruption of hope in her chest. He threaded his fingers through her wet hair and held her face still as he scanned it with his eyes. He seemed to want to say something, but didn't. Instead, he placed her head on his chest and cuddled her.

Strangely, she didn't feel disappointment that the words were not there. What she felt was something much more valuable right now, something more important to her than words could ever be.

She felt cherished.

"Come on," he said as he switched off the stream of water. "Before we're both waterlogged."

Johanna smiled at him as they stepped out of the tub. As Michael wrapped a bath towel around her, she grabbed another and proceeded to dry him.

"Stay still," she said, and he did.

Michael's throat was tight with emotion as he let Johanna efficiently rub the towel over his skin. He felt himself shake inside. This wasn't just about sex anymore. Or about Jeff. The thing he'd feared most had never materialized. No ghost had come between them in bed last night; no specter of his brother hung between them now. He wasn't feeling lust anymore, though he knew at any given time with Johanna that feeling could return in force. No, what he was feeling now was something else, something more, something so powerful and totally unfamiliar that he could give it no name.

Yes, he could. It was *love.*

He was just about to tell her so when there was a knock at the door.

"Mmm, breakfast!" Johanna said. "I'll get it." She quickly donned one of the monogrammed terry-cloth robes the hotel provided. "Coming," she called, wrapping a bath towel around her head as she made her way to the door.

"Good morning, ma'am," the waiter said, rolling the serving table into the center of the sitting room.

Johanna rummaged through her purse for a tip and signed the bill as the waiter meticulously arranged the table and chairs. He popped the bottle of champagne and mixed mimosas in the flute glasses, set the table and placed a singular red rose in full bloom in a crystal vase at its center.

She smiled and thanked him, shutting the door behind him just as Michael entered the room wearing a similar terry robe.

"Nice," he said as he placed a kiss on the tip of her nose.

He lifted one of the flute glasses and handed it to Johanna, then took the other for himself.

"To us," he said, and Johanna's heart blipped in her chest.

"Yes. To us."

They sipped the bubbly drink and set the glasses down on the table. Michael held out a chair for her, and she made a gracious curtsy with her robe to thank him.

"Food!" he said, lifting the metal covers from the plates.

Johanna broke off a small piece of omelet and fed it to him, then Michael did the same for her. The two stared at each other, smiling, their mouths full of food, when another knock sounded.

"Who can that be?" Michael asked, rising to get the door.

"Maybe the waiter forgot something," Johanna said, patting his hand to stay put. "Eat your breakfast. I'll get it."

"No, I'll get it," he said.

They looked at one another, and the challenge was set. Like two children, they dodged each other, then lunged for the door at the same time, laughing as they fell against it. The towel unraveled from Johanna's head and fell to her feet.

"You're crazy," Michael said as he tried to catch his breath.

"Look who's talking," Johanna answered, wrapping her arms around his neck.

He kissed her as he opened the door.

"Morning!" Donna Sue and Jack Larsen stood in front of them with big smiles on their faces.

Dumbstruck, Michael and Johanna stared at the older couple for an awkward moment.

"Jack! Donna Sue! What a surprise," Michael said, recovering first. "Come on in."

Johanna quickly disentangled her arms from his neck and picked up the discarded towel from the floor as the two stepped into the room.

"We were just on our way to check out and thought we'd say goodbye one more time," Jack said.

Johanna grabbed the lapels of her gaping robe and clutched them together. "How wonderful!" she said with a forced smile.

"Oh, Jack, I told you we should have called first. Looks like we interrupted their...breakfast."

Michael looked from the red-faced Johanna to the Larsens and back. Cheshire-cat smiles graced the faces of the older couple.

"Well, we had a short and sweet breakfast meeting early this morning, and my team is just thrilled you're with us. Thought I'd let you know."

Michael straightened his robe as if it were a tailored suit jacket. "I'm happy to hear that, Jack. I'm looking forward to working with them."

Johanna moved next to him, a smile plastered on her face. They looked like barefooted bookends in matching robes, both still wet from what was obviously the same shower. All Johanna wanted to do was dig a hole through the floor and climb in.

Jack stepped forward and handed Michael a briefcase. "Just some papers you need to go over. No rush, now. Enjoy the rest of the weekend. I'll call you on Monday."

Michael reached for the briefcase. "Sure thing, Jack."

"Well, we'd better be going," he said to Donna Sue, who was giving a maternal pat to Johanna's cheek.

"I see you took my advice," Jack said to Michael in a low voice.

"About . . . ?"

Jack nodded toward Johanna. "You know. . . ."

"Yeah," Michael said, smiling. "I guess I did.

"Well, keep taking my advice, and we'll get along just fine."

"Jack, let's go and leave these two alone."

"Right. Got a plane to catch."

The two couples said their goodbyes. Michael shut the door behind them, then turned and leaned against it to face Johanna. "I *don't* believe it," he said.

"I'm so embarrassed."

"Me too."

They looked at each other for the longest second, and then burst out laughing.

"Did you see the look on Donna Sue's face when you opened the door?" Johanna asked.

"No, I was too busy looking at Jack looking at you in that bathrobe!"

"Oh, well," Johanna said. "At least Donna Sue got her wish."

"Her wish?"

"Yes, she gave me a bit of advice, and last night I took it."

"You mean . . . ?"

"Yes."

Michael shook his head. "Jack gave me the same piece of advice." He looked into her eyes. "You beat me to it," he said softly.

"Leave it to a woman."

He opened his arms to her. "*My* woman."

She glided into her spot in the center of his arms, the one that was made for her. Michael slanted his head and kissed her. She leaned into him, wrapping a leg around his ankle.

"I have a great idea," he said.

"What?" she asked between kisses.

"What do you say we pack up?"

Johanna looked into his blazing blue eyes. "And?"

"And . . . go home."

Johanna's eyes sparkled as she nodded. "Oh, yes," she said. "Let's go home."

She moved into his room. There was no need for any pretense anymore. They went to bed together each night and woke up in each other's arms every morning. Johanna was so much in love she couldn't see, think or hear anything that didn't have something to do with Michael. And most of all, she could not remember another time in her life when she was this deliriously happy.

There was only one small cloud on her horizon. She had yet to tell Michael about what had really happened on the night of Jeff's fatal accident. She told herself a million times that it didn't matter, he'd never know, but her innate sense of right and wrong, her basic honesty, pricked her conscience, and she knew that sooner or later, she'd have to tell him the truth.

Everything was so wonderful right now, yet so fragile. She had a fear that her admission could bring it all crumbling down around her. What if he didn't understand? What if he asked her to leave? Her heart pounded with the thought. Oh God, she prayed, don't let it happen like that. Please make him understand, make him know that I only did it to protect his family.

But that wasn't entirely true, and she had to first accept that fact. She had also wanted to protect herself. She had carried the burden of guilt about that night for so long, it was a part of her, and she guarded it as ferociously as she did any other secret in her heart.

But if she was going to have any sort of life with Michael, it was time to let go, to tell him the truth and face whatever consequences followed.

They were in love. She knew it in her heart, though he still hadn't said the words. Each night he'd come so close to it, Johanna knew it was only a matter of time before he did. And what would she say when he declared himself? Would she say, "I love you, too, Michael," as she longed to do? Or would the words stick in her throat, unable to get through the roadblock of the lie she'd kept so long?

Johanna climbed the stairs to check on Michael. It was Saturday morning, and she'd awakened before him, letting him sleep late and catch up on some much-needed rest. She tiptoed passed the bed and into the bathroom, placing fresh towels on the rack. Temptation called, though, and she leaned over Michael to check on him before making her way back out of the room.

He was lying on his side, hugging the pillow, his hair falling over his forehead and one eye. She reached out to push it back, but before she could touch him, his eyes opened.

"Hi," she said softly.

Without saying a word, Michael reached out and pulled her onto the bed. Replacing the pillow with her, he hugged her to him, burying his face in her neck. Johanna smiled as she caressed the back of his head. Michael looked up at her, his face sleepy, warm, his eyes alive with something she could only term love. Johanna's insides twisted with the wish, but before she could even think it through, he said it.

"I love you."

Stunned that her train of thought had suddenly become a reality, Johanna didn't know how to respond, telling herself instead that he really hadn't said the words, that she was hearing things, that her imagination was working overtime. Nervously, she pulled away from him. "I'll get breakfast."

"Johanna," he said softly, "come here." Reluctantly, she returned to the edge of the bed. Michael pushed himself up on his elbow, beckoning her with his hand. "Closer."

She complied, but held herself stiff.

"What's wrong?" he asked.

"Nothing."

Michael raised his eyebrows. "Nothing? I tell you I love you, you pull away from me, and you say that's 'nothing'?"

Johanna laughed a nervous laugh. "Michael, I . . ."

He sat up, the sheet falling to his waist, baring his chest, and her eyes fixed on the view. "You what, Johanna?"

"I . . ."

"Say it."

"I can't."

Michael's eyes narrowed in a combination of shock, disbelief, as well as a little fear. "Don't you love me, Johanna?"

She saw the hurt, and her heart swelled in her chest. "Oh, Michael," Johanna said as she jumped off the bed and moved to the fireplace at the other side of the room.

"Johanna, what the hell is wrong?"

She turned to look at him. "I have something to tell you."

"Come here and tell me."

"No, I'd rather stand here."

"What's this about?"

"Jeff.

"I thought we settled all of that. What about Jeff?"

"About his accident.

"Yes . . . ?"

"I could have prevented it."

"Don't be absurd, Johanna. How could you have stopped it? You weren't even in the car with him. He was killed by a drunk driver."

"No."

"No, what?"

"Jeff wasn't killed by a drunk driver. He hit a tree. *He* was the drunk driver."

"What are you saying?"

"I'm saying I knew he'd been drinking, and I let him take the keys and drive off. We were having an argument."

"About?"

"Us. Or the end of us. I'd asked him for a divorce."

Michael got out of bed. He disappeared into the closet and lifted a pair of jeans off the rack, then slipped into them without zipping them. He walked over to Johanna and took her by the hand. She was shaking. He urged her forward and sat her on the edge of the bed next to him.

"Tell me all of it. From the beginning."

Johanna took a deep breath. "Jeff and I weren't sharing the same room anymore. He was out more than he was in. He had a friend . . ."

"Female?"

"Yes. But it's not what you think. We'd not been . . . intimate . . . for years. I had no problem with it. But I did want to end the marriage. He came home that night and had a few beers. It was pretty obvious that he'd had a few before he arrived, but I was too busy worrying about what I was going to say to him to notice how many more he drank." She flexed her hands in her lap and stared at them. "I told him I wanted out, and he shrugged it off." She looked up, but not at Michael. "You see, we'd had this conversation many times before, and I always gave in. Jeff thought this was just another one of those times." She paused and turned to him, her eyes wet with tears. "It wasn't. This time I meant to go through with it."

"And Jeff argued with you."

"Yes. He ranted, raved, screamed, had one of his usual temper tantrums. But this time I wasn't buying it. By the end of the night, he swore he would fight me in court. I don't think he even realized what he was saying. He grabbed the keys and stormed out. I let him." She breathed in deeply, then exhaled slowly. Her hands formed fists, and she struck out at her knees. "I've gone over it and over it a thousand times in my mind. I could have taken the keys away from him. I could have hidden them when he wasn't looking. I could have done a dozen different things to stop him from leaving that night, but I did nothing. He took off in a rage. An hour later, I got the phone call."

"Why didn't you tell us?"

"I couldn't!"

She stood up and returned to the same spot by the fireplace, away from him, away from what she was sure would be an accusing look in his eye. Running a hand into her hair, she held it back from her face as she spoke. "I knew how your parents felt about Jeff. At first I thought, 'What's the point of upsetting them more than they already are? Let them think it was someone else's fault.' But what I was really trying to hide was that it was *my* fault. All mine." She paused. "They—you—trusted me to take care of him. I failed Jeff. I failed all of you."

Michael sat for a moment to absorb what she had said. Strangely, he was not surprised by the truth about Jeff's accident. He'd always had a feeling that there had been something more to it, but it upset Johanna to talk about it, and he had chosen not to pursue it. What did surprise him was her guilt, her feeling that she'd failed all of them. As if it were her fault he died.

He rose and walked over to her. "Look at me," he said. She lifted her eyes to his. "You must hate me."

"You little fool," he said gently. "To think that I could ever hate you, for any reason." He cupped her face in his palms. "I love you, Johanna."

"Even after what I've just told you?"

"*Especially* because of what you just told me." She wrinkled her eyebrows in question, and he leaned down to plant a kiss on the tip of her nose. "Don't you think my parents and I knew Jeff as well as you? Don't you think we knew how he depended on you? Jeff held on even after it was obvious the marriage was over. To Jeff, you and his music were one. Without you, the dream would die." Michael stroked her face. "My parents were grateful to you... but never, ever did they feel that you were responsible for Jeff. He was a grown man, Johanna. They would never blame you for what he did."

"And you?"

"Least of all me. I told you once before that we sometimes do things we wish we could turn the clock back and do over. But hindsight is wonderful. Could you have stopped Jeff that night? I don't know. Maybe. But maybe not."

"I wish I could believe that."

"Believe it. I've lived with that question for more than ten years."

"What question?"

"Should I have stepped aside and let Jeff have you? Or should I have told my brother how I felt about you, told him that I wanted you, too. Told him that I'd fight for you."

"Oh, Michael, you *did* feel something for me back then."

"More than I knew at the time. It ate at me for years. I was angry. I wanted you for myself. I wanted it so badly that I stayed away from my brother and from you. I was jealous of him for having what I wanted. You want to talk about hiding? I hid behind a wall of indifference to you all these years because I couldn't face that truth—that I made a mistake by letting you go in the first place." He tightened his grip on her. "Jeff's death cleared the way, but not our consciences. That's what made it so hard for us to be together. But we have something stronger than guilt, Johanna. We have love."

The tears on her face wet his cheek as he kissed her deeply. Without another word, he led her to the bed and pulled her down on top of him. With a hunger that defied reason, they stripped the clothes from each other and, without preliminaries of any kind, came together.

"I love you," he said to her with each thrust of his body. "I want you with me. Forever, Johanna. Say it."

"Forever," she whispered into his mouth as he slanted his head and kissed her again.

Like a summer squall, the storm between them raged and fell with alarming speed. She called out his name, and he gave her all he had, surrendering himself, his life, his very soul to her.

When it was over, they kissed, a slow, long, poignant kiss now clean and clear of any of the debris of the past.

"Marry me, Johanna...."

"Yes...."

His eyes sparkled. "Babies. I want lots of babies."

She smiled. "Like Donna Sue said, we have to fill up those empty rooms."

Michael's eyes turned serious. "You do love me, don't you, Johanna? You haven't said it."

"Oh, Michael, my darling." Johanna lifted her hand and gently pushed the hair from his forehead. "Sometimes I think I've loved you forever."

Michael cupped her face in his hands and kissed her, knowing in his heart, his soul, that she was no longer his brother's wife.

She belonged to him.

* * * * *

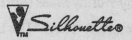

The Loop™

Is the future what it's cracked up to be?

This February, find out if Emily's marriage
can be saved in

GETTING OUT: EMILY
by ArLynn Presser

When Emily said "I do," she had vowed to love Marsh
forever. And she still loved him, but marriage wasn't
as easy as her parents made it look! Getting married
so young had been hard enough, but now that she
was going back to school, things were getting even
worse. She wanted to meet new people and try
different things, but all Marsh wanted to do was
cocoon! Suddenly the decisions that had seemed so
right just a few years ago seemed totally wrong.

The ups and downs of life as you know it continue with

GETTING AWAY WITH IT: JOJO
by Liz Ireland (March)

GETTING A CLUE: TAMMY
by Wendy Mass (April)

Get smart. Get into "The Loop!"

Silhouette®

is

DIANA PALMER'S
THAT BURKE MAN

He's rugged, lean and determined. He's a
Long, Tall Texan. His name is Burke, and he's
March's *Man of the Month*—Silhouette Desire's
75th!

Meet this sexy cowboy in Diana Palmer's
THAT BURKE MAN, available in March 1995!

Man of the Month...only from Silhouette Desire!

A new series from Nancy Martin

Who says opposites don't attract?

Three sexy bachelors
should've seen trouble coming
when each meets a woman
who makes his blood boil—
and not just because she's beautiful....

In March—
THE PAUPER AND THE PREGNANT PRINCESS (#916)

In May—
THE COP AND THE CHORUS GIRL (#927)

In September—
THE COWBOY AND THE CALENDAR GIRL

Watch the sparks fly as these handsome hunks fall for
the women they swore they didn't want!
Only from Silhouette Desire.

Robert…Luke…Noah
Three proud, strong brothers who live—and
love—by

THE CODE OF THE WEST

Meet the Tanner man, starting with
Silhouette Desire's *Man of the Month* for
February, Robert Tanner, in Anne McAllister's

COWBOYS DON'T CRY

Robert Tanner never let any woman get close
to him—especially not Maggie MacLeod. But
the tempting new owner of his ranch was
determined to get past the well-built defenses
around his heart.…

And be sure to watch for brothers Luke and Noah,
in their own stories, COWBOYS DON'T QUIT
and COWBOYS DON'T STAY, throughout 1995!

Only from

SILHOUETTE®

Desire®

Hearts of Stone

Three strong-willed Texas siblings whose rock-hard
protective walls are about to come tumblin' down!

A new Silhouette Desire miniseries by

BARBARA McCAULEY

March 1995

TEXAS HEAT (Silhouette Desire #917)
Rugged rancher Jake Stone had just found out that he
had a long-lost half sister—and he was determined to
get to know her. Problem was, her legal guardian and
aunt, sultry Savannah Roberts, was intent on keeping
him at arm's length.

August 1995

TEXAS TEMPTATION (Silhouette Desire #948)
Jared Stone had lived with a desperate guilt. Now he
had a shot to make everything right again—until the
one woman he couldn't have became the only woman
he wanted.

Winter 1995

TEXAS PRIDE
Raised with a couple of overprotective brothers,
Jessica Stone *hated* to be told what to do. So when
her sexy new foreman started trying to run her life,
Jessica's pride said she had to put a stop to it. But her
heart said something *entirely* different....

HOS-1